TEE & A

GEORGE ONSTOT

ISBN: 0991939603
ISBN-13: 978-0-9919396-0-2

ALSO BY GEORGE ONSTOT

Bullies on Juice
Macho Fellows
Hole in One

1

I looked at that golf mum, and my lecherous Canadian penis sprang erect. It thought, *There's no way that woman can have an eighteen-year-old daughter. Just no way.*

She wore a short dark skirt that showed off curvaceous golden legs meant to spread in bed and a cream-colored blouse covered her youthfully jutting breasts.

Of course, this happened to be the humble opinion of me, Clancy Wasserman, sportswriter.

I had come to this tournament looking for girls. As a sports journalist who covered golf, I had gotten sick of writing about Tiger Woods, so I started checking out the ladies. After a couple of decades of watching Tiger humiliate the competition so routinely that those guys went there *expecting* the degradation and therefore weren't terribly bothered by it, my job

PUBLISHED BY
THE GOOD WORD

FOR D.J.

became tedious. The other golfers seemed content merely to show up, finish second or twelfth or twenty-second, collect their money and give me insipid quotes.

I had also heard that the LPGA had improved, or at least changed. Just as women's tennis had fewer Martina and Billie Jean non-males than before, golf now had some cuties who could swing their clubs and turn men on.

Anyway, on this balmy day, the lady in the dark skirt had a shoulder bag banging against her hip and a pair of white plastic sunglasses that slid down her nose a bit. Her fair hair tumbled down her shoulders and she tugged at it like a movie star. She looked at the leaderboard, then looked away, and looked at it again.

So far as I knew, she could have been one of the golf sisters, cousins or aunts. I asked one of the obvious golf mums about this beautiful stranger.

I had options about whom to ask. Some women sitting nearby were clearly golf mums. I knew they were because they looked like aging cuties. They had brought their own seats and binoculars, and kept studying papers the breeze tried to snatch away.

I sauntered over to a lady who looked especially genial and approachable. I introduced myself as Clancy Wasserman, badass hotshot sportswriter from the Great White North.

"I'm Dawn Baxter," she said, a passably pretty woman in her early forties.

"Any idea who *she* is?" I pointed at the lady in the plastic sunglasses.

"Her?" Dawn made a face, as if we were at a Lakers game and I hadn't yet figured out who Kobe Bryant was. "That's Helene Vachon. Are you really a sportswriter from Canada?"

"I'm afraid so. Please fill me in."

"Helene is Vicki Vachon's mother."

That didn't really tell me much. I had heard of Vicki Vachon and knew that she was the newest darling of women's golf. At eighteen, she could murder the ball down the fairway, chip it out of sand traps or coax it in from six feet away. She was from Lightning Bay, Ontario, which called itself a suburb of Toronto, and had traffic jams to rival those of Chicago or Los Angeles.

Vicki, a pro since the previous year, had already won over a million dollars in LPGA events. This year, she had come in second a couple of times and pocketed a couple of hundred thousand dollars. Well, if Vicki was under twenty, her mum couldn't have been forty, and could have passed for thirty.

"Did you notice," Dawn Baxter whispered, "Helene's shoulder bag? It's no knockoff; it's the real deal. A Versace. Vicki must have spent a ton of bucks on that thing."

"Reminds me a bit of some of the things Tiger Woods has bought himself over the years," I whispered back. Then, "Is there a Mr. Helene Vachon anywhere? She seems to be alone."

"They're divorced. He's a prick."

I smiled. "Good to know. Thanks for your time."

I went over to where Helene Vachon stood, thinking that, for me, the world of women's professional golf just became much more attractive.

As a sportswriter and amateur golfer, I had cared very little about women's golf. I thought of plump old women in dowdy apparel taking forever and a day to make the simplest putts. I wanted to shout, "Put it in there, Granny! The sun's going down!"

I concluded that Helene Vachon and I should meet, since I wrote sports stories that seemed to be on everyone's iPad and could help her daughter's very young golfing career.

Also, I had been dateless for a few years, divorced for four and horny as a ram. My first wife, Nicole, a reporter for *The Bayporter*, had given up on me because she had met an accountant who could give her things and take her to places I could not; my second missus, Elizabeth, had found me financially impotent, too.

I did my best not to take my two failed marriages seriously, or at least personally. Nicole and Elizabeth were pretty women who wanted professional men who made big money, and very few reporters fit that description, so those women had rejected my paychecks, not me. I took some comfort in perceiving my divorces that way, just as I had convinced myself that God had shown us His fallibility by refusing to let our household pet live to be fifty or sixty.

Nicole and I got along better after splitting up. In most ways she was a very desirable woman, and I could hardly blame her for wanting a man who made good money and stayed home. I had spent much of my married life interviewing jocks on flights or catching planes to hook up with superstar athletes and write about them.

Wife Number Two, Elizabeth, had charmed me with her fashionable clothes and clever sense of humor. Alas, not until we were married did I learn about what a soulless, demanding, profligate harridan she could be. When angered, she threw punches, and she landed some good ones. I covered up, and she pounced my arms till they were blue and welted. She left me for a lawyer, and I wanted to shake his hand and say, "You can have her, pal. Just watch out for her left jabs."

2

"I need you," my editor had said over the telephone, "to fly down to Los Angeles and drive out to a ladies' golf tournament in a section of southern California that most people don't know about. You will stay at a hoity-toity new place called Idyllic Village. It's billed as 'an exhilarating new vacation destination.' Well, aren't they all?" He chuckled. "I've never actually been there, but from what I understand, it's located way out there in the desert, probably not too far from where the Manson Family hid out from the cops all those years ago.

"You should rent a Cadillac or something, because you'll need to be comfortable as you drive through the desert. Once you get checked in at Idyllic Village, you will start covering the Hottie Classic."

"What the fuck," I asked, "is the Hottie Classic'?"

"Hottie," he said, "is a brand of women's jeans. The jeans make big, flabby bums look small and cute.

This is Hottie's first golf tournament."

"Why," I asked, "do they call it the Hottie Classic when this is their first year?"

"Gee, Clancy, I don't know."

By the time I arrived there, the tournament had already begun, and this LPGA event would receive page-seven coverage in a handful of small online news services. The only people who really cared about its outcome were the players themselves, their mums and dads. I had a few days and fifty-four holes to cover.

At the front desk, they had given me a press badge, media kit. After going to my room and taking a shower, I went out to check out the Hottie Classic.

The media kit said that Carver and Moe Warner of Malibu had built Idyllic Village as the fulfillment of a lifelong fantasy. They hired Miles O'Connell, "the celebrated San Francisco architect," to design "thirty-six holes of fabulous golf." They had two courses: Village, the site of the tournament, and Bungalow, the easier course.

I knew right away what Miles O'Connell had sold Carver and Mo: a course full of man-made lakes, ponds and sand traps and palm trees flown in from elsewhere. Also, O'Connell, lacking inspiration, had probably just gone online, gotten the layouts of the sixth at Pebble Beach or the tenth at Augusta, and—*voila!*—his work was done.

I knew that Carver Warner had been rich ever since British Petroleum had bought the Warners' company, Royal Oil. He had probably built Idyllic Village out of sheer boredom.

But now I stood out there, gazing at Helene Vachon's lovely bum and wondering if this divorced golf mum had any room in her life for a pushing-fifty, twice-divorced sportswriter from Bayporte.

I felt tempted to go up to her and make a corny joke, but maybe she wouldn't go for it, so I tried pretending I was a normal person.

"Hello," I said, "I'm Clancy Wasserman from *Canadian Sports* magazine. I understand you're Helene Vachon—Vicki's mum."

She shook my hand and said, "Yes, I'm Helene Vachon. I'm afraid I don't read *Canadian Sports* magazine."

I shrugged. "Neither do I. I just write for it."

She laughed. "But you make a living, so you

obviously have readers."

"A few. Mostly because we're online and have an app, so everyone can download us onto their iPads and read us whenever they get sick of the eight million other items they've downloaded."

"I'm embarrassed to admit not reading it, especially since Vicki and I are from Quebec. We should support Canadian publications." She paused. "My iPad is in my suite. Before I go to bed tonight, I should subscribe to *Canadian Sports*. What sort of stuff do you write for them?"

"Heavy, heavy stuff. I feel some Pulitzer-quality prose forming in my brain, but the muse is on her coffee break or something and I need the little bitch to help me. As I say, people download so much reading material that they forget what they read and who wrote it. People have said to me, 'I read your story in *Golfer's Digest*,' or, 'I caught your article in *Golfers' World* and I'll say, 'Nope.' Then they say, 'Yeah, it was *Canadian Sports*,' and I'll say yes. Then they'll want to know what I do for a living, because writing about sports can only be a hobby."

"You write about sports in general, hey? Not just

golf?"

"All sports, especially if there's some sort of Canadian angle to it. I used to do men's golf, but it got to the point where we'd asked Tiger Woods every question except for how often he took a dump, so we decided to check out ladies' golf and see what was going on."

"The LPGA needs to be promoted," Helene said. "Don't you like Tiger? He's got the cutest ass."

"If you say so. There are some cute asses out here that I'm more interested in."

She smirked. "Why you dirty old man."

"That's me." Then, "I like Tiger, but he's had his career at a time when there's no competition, just a bunch of professional losers. They really got to me. Those professional losers just show up, do their unremarkable best and collect whatever prize money they've won. The sponsors drool all over the losers during the photo opportunities. It's like America is rewarding mediocrity."

"You call them 'losers' even though they've had some success in the PGA?"

I nodded. "The PGA Tour today is full of losers.

Years ago, there were guys you could really respect: Nicklaus, Trevino, Crenshaw and a bunch of others. But not now. Today, the losers get paid for showing up and failing to win. All the while, they piss and moan about the golf course and clubhouse, and they hint that if things don't improve, they won't be back. They don't bother with each other or the press. All they care about are coaches, shrinks and famous sports reporters on TV." I sighed. "It's all tedious and depressing."

"You should write about that."

"I do. All the time. But the dreariness continues," I told her.

3

"I have written," I told her, "that the PGA needs to have a major collapse before it can rebuild itself. People laughed at me."

"You were smart," Helene said, "to be so frank about matters. But you do sound bitter, Mr. Wasserman."

"Call me Clancy. I'm not bitter, just cynical. My cynicism comes from being around pro golf for so long. I also get amused when I see these professional losers out there, because I know I'll still be out here covering the sport long after the losers have disappeared and can't understand wants a cell phone picture with them."

Helene looked at me for a bit, then looked down and away, as if trying to decide if I was talking shit or sense. Finally, she looked down the fairway and said, "There's my superstar. She looks pretty intense, eh?"

Vicki Vachon, her mum's superstar, stood nearly a couple of hundred feet away. Her partner for the moment, one of the many Indians and Pakistanis on the LPGA Tour, had landed in the sand. A person looking at the LPGA scores would think he had come across the cast of a Bollywood movie.

Vicki took a firm, smooth swing at the ball and it flew in our direction. It struck the edge of the green, rolled towards the center and stopped maybe half a dozen feet from the hole.

"Yeah!" Helene yelled through cupped hands. "You go, girl!"

Helene and Vicki looked more like siblings, I said to myself as Vicki marched up towards us. Tall, golden-haired, her goodies just where they should be; and she had that sense of invincibility all winners seemed to possess. Some very good genes in that young lady. I could see where she got some of it. I bet her father, whoever and wherever he was—and whatever his flaws—he wasn't exactly poor, dumb and ugly, either.

"That girl," I said, "looks like she could break hearts and drive strong men to drink if she wanted to."

"What a sweet thing to say," Helene muttered.

"I was paying her a compliment." Then, "I'm glad she's using a normal putter. Some of the golfers today use clubs that don't look like anything made for golf."

Vicki had on skimpy white shorts and a clingy red top that confirmed the presence of zero body fat. With no particular expression on her face she tapped the ball, watched it drop into the cup, did the most modest fist-pump I had ever seen and headed over to the next tee. She paid no attention to her cheering mother.

The mum reached into her shoulder bag, pulled out a package of Player's Lights and lit one. "Cigarette?" she asked me.

"No, thanks," I said.

"The better she plays, the more I smoke."

"Those Player's Lights aren't real cigarettes," I told her. "I used to smoke like a chimney, and for a while I liked Pall Malls, the most toxic brand ever. I smoked during dinners, divorces and deadlines. They made me as high as a kite. I would have smoked in the shower if they'd made waterproof Pall Malls."

"Are you a nonsmoker now?"

I nodded. "They've changed the laws. It's

impossible now for people to smoke whenever the cravings start."

"Well, it's good that you stopped smoking."

"What I want to do now," I told her, "is write about Vicki. Who is her agent?"

"We don't have an agent."

"Wow. I would think you two would be fighting them off with a nine-iron. Plenty of them are checking her out and waiting for the best moment to come by and talk you into signing a contract. Agents know that athletes can be very dumb about money and business. So can singers, actors and writers. Vicki is beautiful and successful. She could make some greedy agent a pile of money. Who is her entourage?"

"Me, myself and I. I was a good amateur player years back. But I hear what you're saying about agents. Bert Levenson, Danny Hewitt and had Gresham have given us their business cards and lots of smooth talk."

"I'll bet. Good thing you haven't signed with anyone yet."

"Danny Hewitt," she said, "offered us a few million dollars if Vicki would drop out of high school and turn pro. We felt very tempted but said no, and I'm sure we did the right thing. We wanted her to graduate from high school at the very least, and maybe even go on to university. Vicki's father decided to become her agent and manager, so that he would get the commissions and the money would stay in the family. That arrangement worked out poorly, although he did get some interest from American Express, adidas, Louis Vuitton and a few others while Vicki was still an amateur."

"Did he come out here with you?" I asked.

She let out a contemptuous little laugh. "Vince Vachon and I called it quits a couple of years ago."

"So you two split while he was managing Vicki?"

"He was ripping her off, actually." She glanced in her daughter's direction. "Look, I'm going off to watch Vicki on the next tee. Thanks for the visit, Clancy."

"We'll talk again. I guarantee it."

"By the way, when you came up to me, you knew who I was. Who told you?"

"Dawn Baxter. I asked her and she told me."

Her eyes bugged out. "Really?"

I nodded. "Did she do bad?"

"Dawn Baxter is Winnie's mum. Winnie and Vicki came up at the same time. They have this rivalry going."

"Is Winnie as good as Vicki."

Helene twisted her mouth. "Not exactly. Winnie is a capable player, but she doesn't have the size and strength that Vicki does. Winnie always tries to murder the ball. She doesn't have much self-restraint."

"So Vicki's great and Winnie's not. It must piss them off."

"Oh, sure it does. Winnie can't beat her, no matter how hard she tries. And I guess that's why little fuckin' Winnie tried to kill Vicki last year."

4

In journalism, there are people I call dingbats; and then there those of us who, most of the time, know how to do our jobs.

If a dingbat had stood there talking to Helene Vachon and heard the woman mention that another golfer had tried to kill her daughter, the dingbat would have then asked, "How long has Vicki used her particular brand of golf clubs?"

When Helene told me about that attempted murder, I said, "We really need to talk about that some more."

"You're staying here, right?"

"Yes," I said. "Lucky me."

"We'll keep bumping into each other, Clancy. I'm sure we can put aside a few minutes to talk." Then she hurried off to check out Vicki.

I can't get over how many dingbats have high-paying jobs as sports reporters, and the more they goof up, the bigger their promotions. How did they learn such incompetence? Did their journalism professors in college say, "Shut off your brain before you open your mouth"?

I had learned the word "dingbat" from Phil Ruble when we worked together at *Canadian Sports*. I'd fallen in love with journalism while editing the campus newspaper at Oliver Johnson High School in Bayporte. I knew that journalism, like sports and showbiz, could be brutally competitive and notoriously low paying. I also knew I would love ninety-five percent of it.

Phil, my editor and mentor, had been one of my journalism heroes at Northup University. I also read H.L. Mencken, Mike Royko and Herb Caen, even though their work simply reminded me that they were exemplary, while the rest of us were merely adequate.

I had grown up reading my father, Mack Wasserman. He wrote a daily society-and-gossip column for *The Bayporter*. Dad knew all the nightspots in Bayporte—the Igloo, Roy's on Royal, Rob's on Robertson—and he knew the management, who were kind enough to tell him whenever celebrities came in. Stars visited Bayporte surprisingly often. Dad became famous as the man-about-town columnist who told our city about the time at the Igloo when Miles Davis told a young white couple to fuck off when they tried to say hi to him during an Oscar Peterson piano solo. Dad also wrote about when a heckler got Bette Midler so angry in the middle of her set at Roy's on Royal that she stopped her show and demanded that the jerk get his money back and be removed from the premises.

Dad died at the podium in the Hotel Bayporte's Great Elizabeth Ballroom while roasting a wealthy local entrepreneur. The audience, knowing what a prankster and kidder Mack Wasserman could be, laughed and hooted as Dad clutched his chest and toppled over backwards.

After graduating from Northup, I wrote for the *Bayporte Bugler*. Phil read some of my articles and recommended me to his bosses at *Canadian Sports*. Their veteran staff writer Ty Greer had just announced his retirement, and Phil thought everyone would love seeing if Mack Wasserman's son had inherited any of his father's writing talent.

That happened over two decades ago. By my early

or mid-twenties, I had ended four years at Northup University, where I had covered the Kodiaks, gone on beer busts and attended journalism classes unless a hangover prevented me from doing so. I gave no serious consideration to graduate school, fearing that those wimpy liberal professors would make me think the way they did.

At first, I felt reluctant to replace Ty Greer, who had covered sports for so long and become a Bayporte institution.

"Don't worry about that," said Phil. "Ty knew sports and could write well, but he was the king of dingbats and often couldn't tell the difference between the lead and the bottom. Gary Player could win an open in very dramatic form, and Ty would write about Player's clubs and clothes and how apparel and equipment contributed to a golfer's performance."

. . .

They had put the Hottie pressroom in an isolated part of Icyllic Village. I had finished my third cup of coffee and had just concluded my telephone conversation with Kerry Gaines, *CS*'s new managing editor.

"Clancy, you sports-loving son of a bitch," Kerry had said when he came on the line from his office in downtown Toronto. "Where are you, guy? What are you up to?"

"I'm in southern California, covering the Hottie Classic. But you already knew that."

"I did?"

"Yeah. You thought it was a hell of an idea, Kerry. I'm checking it all out. There are some very sexy women out here. A guy gets horny just speaking their names."

"Ladies' golf, eh?" He paused. "Who gives a shit?"

"They'll give a shit about one girl in particular. Eighteen years old, legs a mile long, heart-shaped ass, gravity-defying titties. She can play golf, too. She could make our cover, or anyone else's."

"Does she have a name?" he asked.

"Vicki Vachon."

...

Kerry had to hang up so he could go to a luncheon with some members of the Avant-Garde Club, an ancient, highly selective Toronto fraternity whose acceptance he had sought for years. After going to some trouble assuring them that he was not Jewish, homosexual, colored or female, he believed they were on the verge of offering him membership. The Avant-Garde Club occupied a big, ivy-colored brick building in a hilly, quaint section of downtown Toronto. It practically shouted at passersby, "You're not good enough for us. Keep moving, buddy."

My conversation with Kerry made me remember how much I disliked working for him.

Kerry, like so many other journalism bosses, had learned most of what he knew from professors who wore beards, suede elbow patches and Wallabees. An infamous dingbat as a staff writer on the magazine, Kerry once asked Michael Jordan, "Why do you shave your head?" as the other reporters rolled their eyes. He said to Wayne Gretzky, "Have you ever had a nose job?"

Kerry Gaines had been my third managing editor since Wim's departure. The other two, like Kerry, had gotten promotions by wearing suits and looking bemused. They perused documents while walking down the hallway, as if headed for a crucial staff meeting instead of the washroom.

Kerry's two predecessors, seeking to pander to the lowest common denominator, had hired every other dingbat who wanted to write, or do goofy layouts, for *CS*. For attempting to make *CS* the laughingstock of North American sports magazines, they received huge promotions. Kerry seemed to want to do as those guys had done, and I predicted that they would kick him upstairs within a year or two.

...

Canadian Sports has its headquarters in Toronto, so they expect me to fly out there for editorial meetings on a regular basis. The company that owns the magazine is RMC, which stands for Rawson Media Corporation. A Bayporte mining tycoon named Rawson decided to buy up obscure radio stations, newspapers and magazines simply because he could do so, and I liked flying out there to his glass skyscraper with its wonderful view of Canada's biggest city.

I felt less fond of the pressroom at the Hottie Classic, probably because I knew nobody. But people came up to me and told me who they were. A few were radio or print journalists; the rest were in public relations.

"Hi," said the nice lady. "My name is Roberta, and I handle public relations for Idyllic Village." No last name, just Roberta. I thought of her as Roberta the Flack. She invited me to a reception in the hotel that evening.

I had stopped attending those receptions several years earlier while covering one of the major tours. The only times I enjoyed myself were when, for the amusement of the others in the room, I mocked a few colleagues who'd made asses of themselves by filing sports reports that were scarcely more than hand jobs for Tiger Woods. Sometimes I felt ashamed of my own profession.

"Don't know if I can make the reception," I told Roberta the Flack. "I have lots of work to do."

"Be there if you can," she replied. "There'll be people you'll want to meet, including Carver and Mo Warner."

5

Two Indians or Pakistanis, Inderjit and Appendy, led with scores in the mid-60s.

"Vicki shot a sixty-eight," Helene said to me.

"Only a couple of shots back. She should be feeling good about that."

"She wants to puke. She said the course was a joke and they should use all of this land for low-income housing."

"Maybe she's right," I said.

We stood just inside the entrance to the reception and looked around. "Nice," she said. "Do you think they could have put any more ice sculptures in here?"

"They'll melt soon," I said, stuffing a caviar-laden toast square into my mouth. "Umm-mmmm."

"Go easy on that stuff. You'll get fat." Helene pointed across the ballroom to the stage, where a band played old music and old people danced. "Isn't that something? To be that age and be able to dance that well?"

"Reminds me of Jack Lalanne," I said, swallowing.

"Who?"

"Jack Lalanne, the exercise guru."

She shrugged. "Never heard of him."

"How about Richard Simmons?"

"Uh, yeah. Everyone knows about *him*."

"Well, before there was Richard Simmons, there was Jack Lalanne. He had his own TV show. He put on shackles and swam across San Francisco Bay while tugging boats." Then, "I guess these dancers are Carver and Mo's friends. The guys have fancy blazers, eh? The women are all dolled up, too."

"They all have nice tans. I like those old dances: the Hollywood Shag and Harlem Shuffle."

I took a long look at Helene in her azure cocktail dress and high heels. "You look magnificent in that dress."

She tugged at it. "What, this old thing?"

"Yeah, that old thing. The way you fill it out—"

"Vicki will be back from the washroom any moment. She wants to meet you, the big famous sportswriter from back home."

Just then Vicki bounded into the room.

"Mr. Wasserman? I'm Vicki Vachon," she said, shaking my hand before her mum could introduce us.

Vicki radiated a winner's confidence, but a mischievous glint danced in her eyes. She wore her blonde hair unpinned, and it cascaded down her shoulders. In her off-white outfit, she looked a vision of creamy, tanned loveliness.

The two Vachon ladies found us a corner table as I headed over to one of the many bars and got our drinks: white wine for Helene, Sprite for Vicki and a double Canadian Comfort over ice for myself.

"A double, eh? No water?" Vicki asked, pointing at my drink.

"I don't want to get gooned tonight," I told her, "but I really couldn't resist drinking someone else's premium liquor. Also, I like to stuff my face with caviar just in case I end up with a rubber chicken that tries to bite me back."

Vicki frowned. "What?"

"He means," said Helene, "that there may not be anything on the menu that he likes, so he filled up on fish eggs."

"Oh."

"I was making a joke," I told her.

Vicki said, "Mum tells me that you're a funny guy, but I don't think sports is a funny thing to cover. Do you agree?"

"Sports is funny, tragic, wonderful, awful and ridiculous," I said. "That's why I love my job. Sports is a metaphor for life."

"And life is a metaphor for sports," retorted Vicki.

"Indeed," I said. "I make fun of stuff for a living."

"Even religion?" Vicki asked.

"Especially religion," I said.

"You shouldn't make fun of that," Vicki said. "Many people believe in it. They get a great deal of comfort from it."

"Maybe that's the reason I make fun of it. People use religion to justify and rationalize their behavior. Millions have died because they believed things that were unacceptable to the powers running the church."

"We're Christians," said Helene. "We go to a Protestant church in Ontario."

"Nice for you." I drained my glass of Canadian Comfort and wished someone, anyone, would come over and offer to freshen my drink.

Vicki said, "Mr. Wasserman—"

"Clancy."

"Mr. Wasserman, do you believe that golf is a difficult, demanding sport?"

"You betcha."

"Yet you make fun of it a lot."

I shrugged.

"He's just a smartass, Vicki," said her mum.

"Too right," I said. "So, Vicki, tell me about you did today."

"I couldn't do anything right."

"It seems to me," I said, "that most people would be very happy to score under seventy, like you did today."

"Yeah, well, 'most people' aren't me. Besides, that course sucks. No eagles out there, just pars and birdies."

Her mum said, "She's feeling low today because she had a few putts that should have gone in. I don't know why they didn't. They just sort of hung out there at the edge of the cup."

I told Vicki that I was from Bayporte.

She brightened up. "That right, eh? I've played at Placid Oaks. Loved it. Did you see Annika Sorenstam and Nancy Lopez play there?"

I nodded. "I wrote it up for the magazine."

"I was there too! Mum took me." She sighed. "Annika and Nancy! Those ladies rule!"

"There are other great women players," I told her.

"No. Annika could kick Nancy's ass, and Nancy could kick everyone else's ass."

"Do you think Tiger Woods could have beaten Ben Hogan?" I asked her.

She shrugged. "Probably. But who cares?"

"Yeah, who cares?" I sat back and stared at my empty glass. Just then I heard a voice behind me.

"Hey! Are you having fun?" asked Roberta the Flack. "Carver and Mo are about to arrive. They're really looking forward to meeting you." To Helene, she said, "Do you mind if I borrow him for a few minutes?"

"Why do you need to borrow him?" Vicki asked.

"So he can go meet Carver and Mo Warner,"

Helene explained.

"That's right," said Roberta the Flack. "Carver and Mo are major investors in Hottie, you know."

"Then you'd better go say hi," said Vicki.

6

Right in the middle of some song, the band stopped and started playing "Hail to the Chief," and in walked Carver Warner in as Uncle Sam, with a top hat and fake white goatee, his red-white-and-blue getup sparkling under the lights. Alongside him, Mo, dressed as Mrs. Sam, wore a white wig. People cheered and clapped and made room for them as they did a couple of quick dance steps.

Roberta the Flack motioned for quiet and said to me, "That's their song. They always do it this way for special events—it's to honor America, the country that's given them far too much." Roberta the Flack seemed friendlier now, much less standoffish, and she told me more than I wanted to know about Carver and Mo Warner.

Carver, the heir to most of the Royal Oil fortune, liked to entertain his community—Malibu—by dressing up as Prince Philip or someone one day each year and tooling around town.

Mo—Maureen—a failed singer, gave up showbiz some decades ago when she met Carver at some hole-in-the-wall nightclub in Manhattan. She and Carver fell in love and married immediately; at her insistence, he hired her bandmates as their bodyguard, driver and personal assistant until, over time, each man died.

Carver, who was quite ordinary apart from being rich, always admired those who were famous for being talented. He had met Dinah Shore at her golf tournament and decided to pursue that sport as a hobby, mostly because it looked so easy. Carver and Mo resented Kraft Nabisco for renaming the Dinah Shore to honor itself.

"But what can *we* do about it?" they asked.

Mo and Dinah had become friends during a party at Dinah's home when the two women sang some songs together. Mo and Carver bought some golf clubs the following day and began yearning for a golf tournament of their own.

Roberta the Flack led me to the Warners' table. Mo climbed on stage uninvited and started singing, not altogether too well, with the band's vocalist, as Carver and another couple watched, listened and smiled. When Mo stopped singing and came down to join us, they had to play a bit of musical chairs to accommodate me at their table.

"Carver, Mo, everyone," announced Roberta the Flack, "this is the famous sportswriter from Canada, Clancy Wasserman."

"How's it goin', eh?" I said with a hearty wave of my hand.

Roberta the Flack smiled, nodded and hurried off.

"The famous sportswriter from Canada," said Carver. "What's the famous sportswriter like to drink?"

I looked to my left and saw a Chinese server standing there. "The famous sportswriter," I said, "would like a double Canadian Comfort over ice."

"Got that, Bruce Lee?" Carver asked the server. "You and Jackie Chan look after the famous sportswriter. In fact, since I wouldn't mind getting shitfaced tonight, bring me whatever you're bringing Clancy."

The server nodded and took off.

Mo leaned over, gabbed my forearm, gave it a hard squeeze and winked at me. Then she let go and looked away, as if the squeeze and wink had never happened.

In my room, I had read Idyllic Village resort's brochure and learned that the resort had an on-premises "College of Cosmetic Refinement" where ladies could get liposuctions, fat transfers, butt tucks and breast augmentations.

Mo had probably gotten all of those once, and some of them twice.

I smiled. "They tell me you are a singer. Do you know any Bruce Springsteen, Ray Charles, Jimi Hendrix?"

A man at the table started snapping his fingers and pointing at me. "Wasserman? I knew of a Mack Wasserman who wrote for that newspaper up there. Kind of a gossip columnist."

I nodded. "My dad."

"So how's old Mack Wasserman doing these days?"

"Not so good," I said. "He dropped dead years ago. But I'll tell him you said hi the next time I visit him at the boneyard."

The two couples ignored me and started talking to each other for a few minutes.

Carver then leaned over to me. "I have to know something from you: Is my course good, or what?"

I shrugged. "Don't know yet. Haven't seen it all. Tomorrow I'll know. It's got bunkers and water hazards, but some of those scores were awfully damn low."

He scowled. "I know. It wasn't supposed to be that way. I wanted my course to be a tough son of a bitch."

"Really?"

He nodded. "Damn straight. I went all the way to San Francisco and said to Miles O'Connell, 'Build me one they'll talk about all over the golf world for a thousand years.' And what do I get? A piece of shit. The girl golfers are out there, making birdies and laughing at me. The girls! They're laughing at me!"

"I think you were asking too much of Miles. I'm sure he did the best he could, but you know how it is today: the best golfers, the high-tech golf balls, the state-of-the-art equipment."

Carver shook his head. "Don't defend Miles. I spent close to ten million on that course. Two million went straight into his pocket. He is an award-winning designer of golf courses. Why? That jackass couldn't design a garden."

"Those girls out there today have been playing golf all their young lives. They are highly skilled and use the very best equipment. It gives them an edge. Maybe the other golfers, like amateurs and weekenders, will find your course much more challenging."

"Maybe," he said. "I doubt it."

Me, too, I thought.

Just then, all the women got up to use the washroom.

"How," Carver asked me, "did girls become such good golfers?"

"How did Tiger get so good? Mum or Dad starts the kid on the golf course or tennis court or ice rink very early on. Today there are big-money opportunities for the big achievers. If the kid is good enough, he or she can provide a good lifestyle for the whole family. Golf academies nurture the kids, too.

College programs improve each year. Plenty of girls grow up with size, strength and excellent hand-eye coordination. Plus, many of them are physically attractive, even sexy. Only a couple have lick-her licenses, if you know what I mean."

Carver sighed and sat back. I sipped my Canadian Comfort over ice and looked around me. Some of the top women's golfers shared a table. From their photos I recognized Kit Manley, Melinda Pardo, Kate McNeney and Linda Rumble.

At another table, Dawn and Winnie Baxter sat together with another mum and girl. Winnie, a bit short and slightly built, just didn't have Vicki's power and would probably find the taller, tougher girl endlessly frustrating to play against. But would Winnie actually try to *kill* Vicki?

I didn't trouble myself to count them all, but figured there must have been forty Indians or Pakistanis on the tour. I checked things out and learned that in India they become pros at fourteen and compete constantly overseas. By they time they start playing in North America, they have already had several years of professional experience.

I looked at Carver, who seemed to be sulking. To cheer him up, I said, "Quite the place you have here. My room is very fancy. Only thing I really need is porno movies on demand."

He frowned. "We have those."

I smirked. "I was just teasing you."

"Well, you're right," he said. "I *do* have quite the place here. I was supposed to have quite the golf course, too, but Miles O'Connell fucked *that* up."

"I can't say it's a bad course after one visit. If the wind starts up and Mother Nature starts sabotaging everyone's game, it could be a very challenging course."

Carver shook his head. "It's fucked. I'll have to have its name changed to Fucked Up Course. My marketing team will have to find a new angle: 'Come to Idyllic Village and play eighteen holes on Miles O'Connell's Fucked Up Course. Even the worst golfer will have the lowest score of his life because the cretin who designed it didn't know jackshit about golf courses.'"

He blew out another huge sigh and stared at his empty cocktail glass. A moment later, the ladies came back and a server materialized. He promised everyone a fresh drink and went away.

I got up and stretched. "It's been lovely seeing you all, but I need to call it a night and do some work back in my room. See you on the greens tomorrow."

On my way out, I looked around for Helene and Vicki, but they had gone too. That figured; they had been bored shitless.

7

Vicki Vachon had looked magnificent in the second half, making easy birdies and taking over the lead.

"She's really shown those Pakis who's boss, eh?" I said to Helene.

"Don't call them that. It's rude."

"I meant it as a term of endearment," I said.

"Anyway, they live here in the States now, so they'll probably become American citizens before long."

"They have American passports and American Express cards, but they don't know enough English to go into a coffee shop and order lunch," I said. "Before long, the white taxpaying American will become an endangered species."

"Is that good or bad?" she asked.

"I think it's bad. My belief is, kill or be killed. It's that simple. A bit of cleansing might be in order. Take all the crazy guys, the suicide bombers, and tie them up together and roast them. It's been known to be high effective."

"You don't think much of diplomacy? Summits? Isn't that what the United Nations is for?"

I nodded. "Oh, yeah. Sit around a table and talk. That'll accomplish plenty. We should have gotten Osama bin Laden to sit down with us. 'Osama, what can we offer you in exchange for your promise to stop doing stuff like what you did to us on Nine-eleven?'"

"Now you're being ridiculous," Helene said.

"Well, maybe that's because the whole damn world is ridiculous."

"Confidentially, I think it's ridiculous that I'm standing here, a zillion kilometers from home, watching my daughter hit a little ball with a thousand-dollar stick so that the ball will drop into a little hole. And pretending that it's the most important thing in my world."

I nodded. "News is ridiculous, too. It's just bullshit. You can never believe what Washington or Wall Street says. In fact, you should just ignore the news altogether. You'll be healthier and live longer."

"Strange thing to say, considering you're a news

reporter."

"Not at all. Sports isn't news. Sports is sports, although sports is even phonier than news. Sports is even phonier than showbiz, too. Maybe that's why I love it so much."

"Well," she said, "don't ever go into politics, because you wouldn't get very far."

"You're right. Politics is for incompetent lawyers who wear ugly suits and live off taxpayers' money. I'm too fashionable and intelligent for that." Then, "Say, you want to grab some lunch?"

. . .

Helene and I walked together behind the ropes of the fairway as we followed Vicki's progress. Across from us stood some fans of Kit Manley, Vicki's golf partner for the day. Kit, a tall, stringy woman pushing forty, had been a pro for some time.

Most of Kit's fans were middle-aged women with short hair, granny glasses and hairy armpits.

"Looks like the nonmales have come out to cheer on one of their own," I said to Helene.

"I'm glad they're here. Kit is a nice lady. She

deserves their support. Don't make fun."

"But making fun is my business," I reminded her. "Anyway, I won't say it again. They outnumber me, and I can tell I'm not their kind."

"Kit," Helene told me, "has been very kind to Vicki. She's explained how the tour works, where to go, what to do, how to prepare for tournaments, and how to deal with obnoxious sportswriters. Nobody else would bother to provide all that information. Vicki and I are grateful to her."

"Just the same," I said, "I wouldn't let Vicki hang out too much with Kit. You know how those nonmales are. They can't resist corrupting tender young maidens. You wouldn't want Vicki to become a dyke, would you?"

Helene guffawed.

"What's funny?" I asked.

"If any woman tried to get too friendly with Vicki, that woman would have to get past Brice Traynor."

Brice, Vicki's caddy, seemed the kind of man one would expect to be Vicki Vachon's boyfriend: tall and tanned, handsome, in awe of his lady love.

"Are they engaged?" I asked Helene. "Is he the

one for her?"

"Oh, she's too young for that. But they like each other a lot. They go out together and watch movies, dance, go for drives. He's been a good caddy and a close friend. Kind of an older brother, too, I suppose."

"Do you have any objection to her dating a caddy?"

"Like I said, it isn't anything permanent. He was a good golfer, too, a few years back. He played at Indiana and wanted to join the Tour. He was good, but not great, so he didn't make the cut. So he said to her, 'I'll become a caddy till I figure out who I want to be when I grow up.'"

"But his sweetie is also his boss," I said. "Is he OK with that?"

"So far, so good."

I smirked. "Maybe I'm in the wrong occupation. Do you think my back is strong to carry a golf bag all day?"

Just then, everyone applauded as Vicki made another birdie.

I wondered if Carver Warner had just seen all

those birdies, and if he knew how much the players and spectators laughed at his multimillion-dollar joke of a golf course. What would he say to Miles O'Connell the next time they spoke, if Miles, the internationally renowned architect, said something really stupid, such as, "So, how do you like the new course I built for you?"

Helene lit a Player's Light. As long as her daughter kept dropping the balls into the holes, she would keep smoking. And if Vicki stopped sinking those putts, Helene would smoke even more.

"This," she said, "isn't the first time Vicki has been this dominant. She put on quite a show at the Buzzard Breath Country Club when she was just fourteen or so."

"I don't know where that is."

"In the Deep South somewhere. We've been to so many of them. I get confused."

We shut up for a bit as Vicki started to struggle and only barely made par for each of the next few holes.

The girl started bouncing around with a smugness and cockiness she hadn't displayed before. She ended up in the sand, then the rough, and managed to put her way out of trouble. Her pretty face blazed red with embarrassment, her pink lips a humorless line, as she bent over to snatch her ball out of the cup, scarcely acknowledging the smattering of applause from the crowd.

I followed Helene over to the next tee and we stood by the ropes as Vicki came along, still thin-lipped with anger over her mediocre moments.

"Looking good out there, Vicki," said the mum with a hearty smile. "Thirty is good. Very good."

"Thirty is bunk," muttered the daughter. "I was after twenty-nine. Should've had it." She spat and added, "I lost it on seven, eight and nine. Shitfuck."

"You're up by a few, you know," said the mum.

"I've already *won* it, Mum." Then she smiled. "Turn in your textbooks and piss on your teacher. School's out."

Kit Manley came by, the two golfers exchanged a high five and went off to the next tee.

"Mum," I said to Helene, "I'm going to go off for a bit and talk to some of these other golfers about Vicki. I want to find out if they think it's true that

Winnie Baxter tried to kill Vicki."

"Bloody fuckin' right it's true."

"Do you want to tell me about it?" I asked her.

She nodded. "We can have dinner tonight."

8

Vicki, ending the tournament with the lowest score in the golf course's young life, bounded into the pressroom to answer questions about, well, everything. But when her answers, due to a brief life spent hitting golf balls and watching TV, became mostly shrugs and smiles, the sportswriters thanked her and moved on to other things.

Helene wiped sweat off her forehead as she stood next to me at the rear of the pressroom. I didn't ask Vicki any questions. Group interviews turn me off; they're filled with dingbats or those who are infatuated with their own voices.

"Quite a round she had, hey?" asked the mum. "A few more birdies. A couple of bogeys, too, unfortunately?"

I looked at her. "Vicki bogeyed? On that course? Really?"

She nodded. "My girl got a bit big-headed out

there. She hit the ball too hard here, then hit it too softly there. Too bad. She really wanted a lower score than she got."

"Hi!" said Roberta the Flack as she approached us in her gray pinstripe suit. I thought that if she ever got tired of public relations, she could become a sexy newscaster on CNN. "Would you like anything to drink?"

"A bottle of water, please," said Helene.

"And yourself, Mr. Wasserman?"

"Please call me Clancy. I'm fine, thanks. I require no refreshments."

"But if you do need anything—"

"I'll come running," I assured her.

"That's what I like to hear." Roberta the Flack smiled and hurried off. When she returned, a moment later, she handed Helene an ice-cold bottle of water.

"Anything at all, Clancy," she said to me as Helene guzzled the water. "First impressions are so vital to us, Clancy. This resort is my home and office, so you might say that I'm *always* available. Carver and Mo prefer to have me close by. Just ask the front desk and they'll take you to my room."

"How thoughtful of them. And you," I said.

She nodded. "We aim to please."

I nodded back.

"Don't be shy," she said. "Speak up if there's anything I can do for you."

She squeezed my arm and winked.

"I promise not to be shy."

Roberta the Flack went away, smiling.

Helene chuckled.

"What's funny?" I asked.

"Roberta the Flack," she said. "She sure takes her job seriously, eh?"

"She's just being conscientious."

"She was seducing you. She failed this time, but she'll try again. I'm a bit of a seducer myself."

"I hadn't noticed. You haven't tried to seduce me."

"No," she said, "but you've been hitting on me plenty."

"Hey?"

"You heard me. You've been trying to get into my pants since the moment we met. Whenever I turn around, I can feel your eyes glued to my bum."

"Nonsense," I muttered. "I'm a sportswriter working on a story. That's all."

"*I* seem to be the story you're working on. Now, hush up. I want to hear what my daughter has to say."

Vicki sat at a table on a platform and, at the sportswriters' request, went into detail about each time she hit the ball. Like most other champions, she agonized over the bunkered balls and missed putts even more than she savored the very fresh memories of those that went in. She sat next to a hard-faced woman in an LPGA blazer who had the task of running the interview session, to the extent that it required running.

Hope, the woman in the blazer, reminded me of a cash-hungry dentist who stands over you and tells you that you need two extractions and three crowns. She tells you so with a poker face even as you can see the dollar signs dance in her eyes.

"What were your feelings about the back nine?" Hope asked Vicki into the microphone.

"Unreal. Outrageous. Wicked."

"In what way?"

"I was a major wrecking machine out there with

my tee ball. My irons were lethal weapons. I was magical on the greens. But I almost dorked it all up with those two boneheaded bogeys. I wanted to finish under sixty *so bad*."

Hope frowned, as we all did. Teenagers' slang could be as frustrating as a foreign language. "Any more questions for Vicki?" she asked.

"Vicki," some sportswriter asked, "what kind of equipment do you use?"

Vicki squirmed a bit. "I haven't signed any endorsement deals."

"Vicki," asked someone else, "how did you like being in that golf academy in the Southeast?"

She beamed. "Oh, it was fantastic. I was there only in the summer, when school was out in Canada. That academy was really expensive. I went there from age twelve to, I guess, sixteen. The instructors were terrific and some of the students were outstanding athletes. Some of the kids have gone on to college sports. Some of them are here at this tournament. They're friends of mine. I thought about going to college instead of turning pro. I got full scholarship offers from the University of Toronto, McGill,

Queen's, Northup."

"Do you still live in Canada?" someone asked.

Vicki nodded. "Part of the year, anyway. My mum and I bought a condo not far from Miami. She's my mentor, confidante and best friend."

"Where are you going next?" another person asked.

"Out to New Mexico next week, then back here for the Dinah Shore." She paused. "Oh, wait. It's not the Dinah Shore anymore, it's the Kraft Nabisco. That's a dumb name for a golf tournament, don't you think?" She made a face, and everyone laughed.

"Where is your father?" was the next question.

"Too personal," Hope interjected. "Anyone else?"

A man's tired voice said, "You're in the lead right now, but the competition is relentless. Do you think you can tough it out and win this thing?"

"Damn right."

"Who are your heroes?" he wanted to know. "Do you have posters on your bedroom walls?"

Vicki pursed her lips. "Mmmm. I've got Bruce Lee up there. Jim Morrison. Celine Dion, Alanis Morissette, Bryan Adams, Michael J. Fox—because they're all Canadians—and that's it for now."

"What kind of music do you like?"

She shrugged. "Classic rock, I guess. I don't have lots of time to hang out and listen to my iPod, so it's hard for me to answer that question."

"What," asked another reporter, "are your plans for tomorrow?"

"To kick some ass, of course."

Everyone laughed.

The same reporter continued with, "You once said—"

"'You once said.'" Vicki giggled. "I love that. You make me sound a thousand years old."

"You once said," the man persisted, "that you want to, and will, become the greatest woman golfer of all time. Is that quote accurate?"

Vicki giggled some more. "Yes, I said that. Not to take anything away from the other girls. There are lots of great ones around. I won't name them because we all know who they are. But I play to win. I say things. I guess I say too much sometimes. But I say what I mean and I mean what I say."

The man said, "Vicki, you're still a teenager, yet you say you aspire to becoming the greatest ever. Aren't you being a bit ambitious?"

"Oh?" Vicki straightened her back and squared her shoulders. "Is it wrong to be ambitious? Should I say, 'I just want to get fat, do nothing and go nowhere; just be'?"

The room rocked with laughter. Vicki herself reluctantly chuckled.

"She sure can talk the talk," I muttered to her mum.

"She can walk the walk, too," the mum shot back.

"Yes, I am still a teenager," Vicki was saying. "But my goals are many and lofty. I want to win everything, everywhere. But you already knew that, didn't you? I want to win millions of dollars, even billions. I want to marry and have children. And if I ever get too old to win at golf, I want to become the very best at my next career, whatever that is."

Some reporter called out, "Want to do a swimsuit commercial?"

Everyone laughed.

"Have your people call mine," Vicki retorted.

Everyone laughed some more.

Hope said, "This session is concluded."

9

"The thing that concerns me most about 'fine dining,'" I said to Helene as we entered the fancy restaurant, "is that I come away from the experience with a full stomach. I don't want to push away from the table and say, 'I've just finished a ten-course meal, and it tasted good, but how come I'm still hungry?'"

Maureen's Cuisine, the name of our restaurant, the best—or at least the most expensive—in Idyllic Village, had plenty of junk strewn about. A little card on our table informed us that Gavin and Issy Antiques of San Francisco was responsible for the junk.

Vicki had opted out of dining with her mum and me. She wanted to eat with her caddy at the delicatessen, then spend the evening with him in the video arcade, zapping bad guys with electronic bullets.

Maureen's menu had many unfamiliar items, so we chose what we knew we would like: chicken for her and salmon for me. Helene washed hers down with white wine and I had a few Canadian Comforts over ice. We had coffee but declined dessert—Maureen's specialty, rhubarb pie.

I told Helene about myself. "I've had luck and success in my job. I've stayed in my profession much longer than other people who got phased out of sports journalism. I've been divorced twice. I quit smoking even though I loved every drag I took. My job and cigarettes sustained me for the longest time. Let's now talk about some stuff that's more interesting than my life."

"The thing you need to remember," Helene said, "is that these girls are isolated and insulated from a very early age. They start being singled out for isolation and insulation practically from the moment they display any golfing ability or interest. Their parents start thinking, 'My kid could win a college scholarship or become a pro golfer! Let's check this out.' The parents start to think that their little girl could put herself through college, especially if those parents are humble folks of modest means, which most of us are. Fathers sometimes give in to the temptations to quit their jobs and manage their daughters' golfing careers. My ex did that."

"Didn't work out so well, eh?"

"It was awful. Alain was a decent sporting-goods salesman who handled all the major brands. But he was a passionate gambler, too, and Vicki was raking in money, so Alain had quite a lot of fun for a little while, but he went bust in Vegas."

"Why did you marry him, then?"

"Because he looked like Kevin Costner. He thought so, too. So did other women, unfortunately." She paused. "Alain quit sporting goods because he found something better: All Sports Management—ASM, I'm sure you know *their* people—hired him when Vicki was fourteen. Danny Hewitt, the boss over there, figured Vicki could get an LPGA waiver to turn pro at seventeen, and that's what happened. Hewitt was convinced that Vicki would be a very attractive commercial entity even when she was that young, and that Danny would represent her. So he paid Alain a hundred thousand dollars a year to 'scout out new talent,' as Danny put it. Alain would escort Vicki to all these junior amateur golf matches and file reports on the most promising girls out there. It was all bullshit, naturally, but the authorities say it's permissible. That's when the trouble began. Alain and I agreed to be very frugal in our own lives and save as much money as we could for Vicki. After all, it really *was* her money. But somehow it ended up in Alain's pocket, then in Steve Wynn's pocket out there in Vegas." She sighed. "But enough about that asshole. Tell me about those two lovelies you divorced."

"Nicole was a reporter at *Canadian Sports*. A pretty girl, but also one of the boys. She liked to drink, smoke and talk sports. But as soon as we became husband and wife instead of just fuck buddies, she decided that, professionally at least, I wasn't any better than she was; therefore, I wasn't quite good enough for her. When I returned from a prolonged road trip, she told me she had met someone else."

She nodded. "So much for Number One. What about Number Two?"

"Elizabeth, a realtor, talked me into buying a Bayporte condo I couldn't afford. Her idea was to marry me and move in with me. She was good-looking, smart, fancy, charming, and she wanted us to be a power couple: The famous sportswriter, who also happened to be the legendary Mack Wasserman's son, and the sexiest, smoothest-talking realtor in town. But one day she looked at us and saw we were a humble couple, not a power couple. Worse than that, her hubby seemed happily humble. She couldn't fix his life because he didn't consider it broken."

"Too bad, eh?"

"Too bad for me. Elizabeth was always meeting new people in her job, and one day she did some business with a man who could offer her the lifestyle I could not. End of story."

"Good riddance to her."

I shook my head. "Here's my favorite Elizabeth story. Towards the end of our marriage, while Elizabeth was covertly scoping out new hubbies, my auntie died and left me something like twenty-three thousand dollars. I put it in the bank and mostly forgot about it, but Elizabeth remembered. She said I didn't give her a wedding ring, and we needed to take care of that. So we went to Boccasio's and she picked out this chunky diamond ring for twenty-one thousand. The following month, she left me."

Helene shook her head. "What a rag."

"I agree."

"You were brave to quit smoking," she said. "I'm not so brave, especially when I'm far from home, watching my kid play high-stakes golf. If I don't get my nicotine fix, I freak out. And since we're in California, where smoking in public is punishable by death blows to the brain, maybe it would be a good idea if we went outside so I can suck on a cancer stick for a little while."

I signaled for our server, Adrian, to bring us the check. He told us that Roberta the Flack would pay it. I simply needed to sign it.

I said, "I can't allow her to do that. My ethics won't accept it. How much?"

He handed me the check. It was just under $800.

I glowered at him.

"The wine," Adrian explained. "The lady had some of the best in our cellar…"

"I didn't even get a sip." I scribbled my name on the check and handed it to him. "Normally I don't allow third parties to buy me fancy dinners, but in this case, you can thank Roberta for her generosity."

Giggling as we hurried outside, Helene lit up a Player's Light. "Eight hundred bucks for dinner! You were smart to let Roberta pay for it."

"I agree. Tell me about yourself," I said. "The brief version."

She blew out a stream of smoke. "I'm an average girl from Lightning Bay, Ontario. Went to Western Ontario College, met Alain, got married, had a kid who's now a golf phenom. I'm what you get when you put an ordinary person in an extraordinary situation. I get overwhelmed. Vicki just deals with it. I envy her."

"Does she get her athletic skill from you or him?"

"Both, probably. Alain and I are both tall and graceful. I got a tennis scholarship; my family had no money, so I had to work and go to school even with the scholarship. I was a waitress and a store clerk. After graduation, I got a job at the Bank of Toronto. I would have stayed at the bank till I turned ninety-nine but Vicki came along and became this golf champ, so I decided to quit my job and travel with my kid, at least for a little while."

"You have a condo in Florida," I said.

She nodded. "A beautiful place not far from Miami. We got it cheap, too, because of the financial downturn and the number of properties that were underwater."

"Tell me more about Vicki."

"These girls, if they're headed pro, start developing their skills at around eleven or twelve." Helene pointed at me. "Did you know that when the kids are that young, their parents are not allowed in the gallery?"

I nodded. "Good. It prevents Mum and Dad from hollering out advice to their small fry."

"Usually it's the father who does that. If he's out there barking, 'Win! Win! Win!' the kid will slack off because the pressure is just too intense. But Vicki looked at golf and said, 'Yeah, I can do this,' and she really has this drive. She'll go out there and hit tee balls regardless of the weather, while all the other girls are hanging out at shopping malls, sitting through bad movies, eating junk food and giving their debit cards a workout at the Gap."

"And checking out the boys," I added.

"And letting the boys *them* out." She rolled her

eyes.

"If Vicki hung out at the mall with the girls," I said, "they would hate her because she would be getting all the attention."

"She gets all the attention, no matter where she goes or with whom."

"Are we going to talk about Winnie Baxter now?" I asked.

"Yes," she said.

We sat on a bench and looked at each other. I felt irritated by the dryness of desert heat. My blood is much too thick for such warm places; I would need to blast the air conditioner into my face all the time, especially during sleep. Helene lit up another Player's Light and it smelled delicious. I wanted to ask her for one, but knew I would hate myself for the rest of the evening if I lit up.

"In India," Helene said, "they have something for every purpose. They have too many rats—of course, even one rat is too many for me—so they make rat poison. That's what they tried to give my daughter."

10

Helene said she bet I had never had heard of a young Indian golfer named Inderjit Dhaliwal.

"You're right," I said. "I'll bet I would have a bitch of a time spelling her name."

"She is from Bombay."

"The movie capital of the world."

"Inderjit and Winnie Baxter became chummy on the tour last year," Helene explained.

"Does Inderjit speak English?"

Helene shrugged. "She's learning."

"Why did those two kids get friendly? Winnie doesn't seem the United Nations type to me."

"I'll tell you about it."

"Is Inderjit out here today? I don't think I would know her if—"

"Shut up already," she said, scowling. "Inderjit isn't here. She's still in India, waiting for an invitation from a sponsor. But when she *does* arrive, I'm sure the authorities will watch her closely."

"So will I, now that I know there may be a juicy little scandal here. I'm a reporter, you know. Winnie Baxter resents Vicki Vachon. Winnie is tight with Inderjit Dhaliwal, who knows how to discreetly poison people."

"You can say that but don't write it."

I arched an eyebrow. "Oh? Are you my editor?"

She shook her head. "You can't write that stuff. It hasn't happened, and you can't write it."

"Who says I can't?"

"The LPGA, for one."

I cackled. "That bunch of wimps?"

"Don't laugh. They have a friend named Uncle Sam."

"Yeah, I've heard of him. Tough old guy. Don't fuck around with him."

Helene nodded. "Uncle Sam doesn't want to embarrass or humiliate an Indian golfer when nothing has been proven about her alleged wrongdoing."

"You'd better run this down for me so I'll have a better understanding of what's going on." I paused. "Damn, I'm craving a smoke."

She took out a Player's Light, stuck it into my mouth and lit it. "All better now?"

I moaned as I exhaled. "Better than sex."

"Better than *safe* sex, anyway." Helene stubbed out her old cigarette, lit herself a new one and sat back. "OK, here it is. Last year in Topeka, at the Fat Freddy's Classic—"

"What the hell is the Fat Freddy's Classic?"

"Haven't you ever heard of Fat Freddy's?"

I shook my head.

"It's a restaurant chain in the Midwest."

"Any good?"

"Yummy. Kind of like Shari's or Denny's, only better. Great pies and sundaes. I bought stock in the company for Vicki."

"OK," I said, "we're at the Fat Freddy's Classic in Topeka. Which golf course?"

"The Vast Plains Country Club."

"Sounds like the kind of place Clint Eastwood would enjoy."

Helene sat and smoked while she watched my face as my mind wandered everywhere. By and by I got it back to where it was supposed to be.

"Shall I continue?"

"Yes, please," I said.

"Winnie had already known Vicki for some time, so she introduced Vicki to Inderjit. 'The Indian girl is lonely and homesick. She needs friends,' Winnie said. Vicki said, 'I'll do what I can for her.'

"Dawn Baxter, Winnie's mum, took the three girls to dinners few times on the tour. Once or twice, I went along, and I remember Winnie and Dawn making some effort to communicate with Inderjit. It didn't mean anything then, but I'm sure I heard Inderjit say the word 'gurr-poon.'

"Vicki had been leading that tournament by a few strokes over Winnie. Although Winnie kept smiling and acting like nothing was wrong, I knew she must have seethed every time she saw Vicki's face or heard her name. Vicki's just such a relentless competitor; she just won't let up, and Winnie was doing her absolute best but it meant nothing. I think Winnie wanted to cry out there out of sheer frustration.

"Well, that evening, I took the three girls out to see some Brad Pitt flick—or was it a Matt Dillon movie? I get those two confused—at a shopping mall close to Vast Plains. Dawn didn't go with us; Winnie said she had to leave town for business reasons, but Dawn usually *never* leaves these tournaments whenever Winnie is number two or three.

"So the girls ended up going to that Brad Pitt movie and I went to the Harrison Ford movie in the same megaplex."

"Were you the only person in that auditorium?" I asked her. "Harrison isn't getting any younger or more popular."

"Brad Pitt is about to turn fifty but the young girls still like him. Anyway, I had been in my seat less than half an hour and really couldn't get interested in the movie, when Winnie came in and got me. She said that Vicki was in the washroom puking her guts out.

"We'd all had popcorn and Cokes, but that was all. Vicki lay on the floor, sweating like a pig, so instead of calling nine-one-one, I got the girls to help me load her into the courtesy station wagon the sponsor had gotten us, and we headed for Topeka General Hospital."

I laughed. "So you drove right up to the ER, and I can imagine your mental state at that time."

She nodded. "Oh, I was quite the raving lunatic. And you know how chaotic most emergency rooms are, so it's not the easiest thing to go in there and say, 'My daughter here is sick, I don't know exactly what's wrong with her, but I need you to check her out *right fucking away*.'"

"I assume they did it, too."

"Oh, yes. They did tests and took blood and stabilized her. Then they dosed *me* up with Ativan!" She sighed. "Vicki was OK soon after that, but she had to withdraw from the competition and one of the Asian girls won it. But I'm going to be very honest with you: I'm thrilled that Winnie didn't win that tournament. Vicki's withdrawal did not help Winnie in any way. Cori Perlich ended up winning the Fat Freddy and Sandra Bertrand came in second. I think Winnie choked and placed tenth.

"The doc at the hospital said that Vicki had probably been poisoned, but he couldn't say what the poison itself was. He guessed it might be strychnine or something similar. He used some long words he knew I couldn't understand, but then he shrugged and said, 'Rat poison. Do they use that kind of stuff on golf courses?'

"And I thought, 'No, but envious competitors might have some use for it.'"

"So," I said, "you're sure that nobody else got sick that night at the movie theater?"

"Absolutely. Just Vicki."

"That must have been an awful night for you."

She shrugged. "Wasn't much fun."

"When did you contact Alain about this?"

"The next day. We were still in the Midwest. I had his cell phone number, so I called him. Naturally, he was in Vegas, sitting by the pool. I ran it all down for him, and do you know what he said? 'Oh, Winnie and Dawn wouldn't do anything to harm Vicki. She probably just ate too much and barfed. You know how she likes junk food. I'm glad she's OK.' A bit later on, I learned that Alain had been banging Dawn for a couple of years. Nice, hey?"

"Well, you married a Kevin Costner lookalike. Shit happens, baby."

11

Helene and I sat there some more on the bench near the hotel's main entrance. People sauntered by; some nodded or smiled, others did not. A server appeared and asked if we wanted anything to drink. He had short blond hair and reminded me very much of Jeff Spicoli, the surfer boy Sean Penn played in *Fast Times at Ridgemont High*. That is, if Spicoli had cut his hair and put on a dress shirt and bow tie.

"I understand," the server said to me, "that you're a writer."

"You understand right."

He nodded. "That's what *I* want to do. My head is full of ideas for movies, TV and novels. I just need to know how to get started. Any tips?"

"Go to college," I told him. "Figure out what kind of writing you want to do, then study your ass off and get a degree. Your professors will help you as much as they can."

"Oh." He frowned and shook his head. "Thanks."

"Don't mention it."

He skulked away.

"You weren't very helpful," Helene murmured.

I smirked. "Did you want me to say, 'Here, kid, take my business card and stay in touch. I'll do my best to get you started in a fulfilling and lucrative writing career'?"

Helene nodded. "Well, it sure as hell would have made *his* evening."

"He said his head was 'full of ideas.' That means he hasn't actually *written* anything yet. He didn't want to hear, 'Go to college and get a degree.' Anyway, you went to the commissioner about what happened to Vicki…"

"She and I left the tour for a few weeks. We went down to our condo in Florida while she chilled out. We hung out on the beaches and in the malls. We did girl things. It's good that we get along so well and can quality time together."

"People mistake you for sisters, too. You're both tall, with cute faces, good boobs and nice bums."

She made a face. "Anyway, we drove up to the LPGA offices. Have you ever been there, Clancy?

Their offices are in Daytona, but if you ripped out the palm trees and tinted windows, those offices could be in any American city."

"Or any Canadian city, for that matter," I said.

"So I met with the commissioner and ran it down for her. I said, 'We have two potentially dangerous girls on the tour. One of them is American and the other is Indian.'"

"Who," I asked, "is their commissioner now? The last time I checked, it was a man, which I makes about as much sense as having a white guy in charge of the NAACP."

"Right now the commissioner is a woman. Her name is Yolanda Rivera. She's been the boss less than a year. She succeeded Carol Williams."

"And what became of Carol Williams?"

"She quit to become Larry King's next wife. Just kidding. I don't know where Carol went, but I do know that the players didn't like her. She was lazy and just wanted to fancy job title and good salary. She was after an even bigger job that paid more money. She used to do some of her job hunting during LPGA office hours."

"Did Carol find that big fancy job she was after?"

Helene shrugged.

"How about Yolanda Rivera?" I asked. "How did the LPGA end up with her?"

"I'm told she was a marketing wizard in New York. She worked for Bonnie Fuller, who had edited *Cosmopolitan.*"

"A marketing wiz, eh? Is that what the LPGA needs right now?"

"I don't know, but what's what they've got." She paused. "So I sat there in Yolanda's office and we talked. Actually, *I* talked. She nodded and took notes. That's not a good thing, when you talk and they don't talk, they just take notes.

Finally she said, 'This is disturbing and difficult to believe, but I guess there is enough circumstantial evidence to merit some concern.'

She said, 'This is a particularly delicate item, especially because one of the individuals is a foreign national. An *Indian* national. But I'll pop on into our legal department and see which way the wind is blowing in terms of treating this as a bona fide criminal issue. I also have friends in Washington,

D.C., so I'll call them about this, too.'

"She ended our meeting by acknowledging that this was something 'we need to talk about again if it doesn't go away on its own.'"

I grinned. "You should have said to the commissioner, 'In much of America, "the bastard deserved it" is considered an acceptable legal defense.'"

"I wish I had said that." She paused and yawned. "Bedtime for me. You don't have to walk me to my room. I'm too tired and cranky to fend off a seduction attempt."

"Then I won't try to seduce you."

"You're trying to seduce me right now."

"You and Vicki are of interest to me only as the subjects of a *Canadian Sports* story," I lied.

"Vicki really needs to win this one tomorrow, to keep up her morale. It will be her first victory since the ugliness I just told you about."

"The thing you just told me about and forbid me to write about."

She nodded.

"I might as well tell you, Helene, that I'm having

breakfast with Dawn Baxter tomorrow. I want to talk to her about some stuff. I hope you don't mind."

"Not at all. Dawn will probably tell you that she and I are very chummy. Ask her about the Cover Girl Open."

"Why? What happened there?"

"That was where Winnie Baxter did the choke of the decade. She was the leader coming down the stretch, but then she psyched herself out. Her hands started to shake and she couldn't make anything go in. She nearly had a crying fit in front of everyone. Hilary Martenson ended up winning, but even Hilary didn't care that much by then. Everyone got so freaked out by Winnie's implosion."

"I won't bring it up."

"Be quiet. It gets worse. Afterwards, Dawn was so enraged that she went into the locker room and started smacking the shit out of Winnie—just started slapping her own daughter and screaming, 'You little cunt! What is your fucking problem?' Hard to believe, eh?"

"People get crazy over money," I said, "especially when they don't have lots of it, and they're very close to getting lots of it, and they end up watching someone else get it. Did that slapping incident get any coverage in the media?"

"No. I wasn't there, so I didn't personally witness it, but Kit Manley saw it all and told me about it. Kit couldn't believe that Dawn wasn't barred forever from LPGA events."

"I assume that Yolanda Rivera, the commish, knew about it."

"Oh, yes. She said, 'Let's bury this incident for the good of the tour.' That was Yolanda's first big decision as boss. 'Let's call these outrageous and humiliating occurrences "internal matters" and pretend that they don't exist.' That seems to be her policy."

We had reached Helene's room. She clasped the key card and looked up at me. "Even if you were trying to get in my pants—"

"Who, me?"

"Yes, you. And even if I were wanting to let you do just that, I couldn't."

"Really? Why not"

"Because Vicki would be sleeping a few feet

away."

"What if we moaned really quiet?" I asked.

Helene stifled a laugh. "See you tomorrow, Clancy. Hope Dawn doesn't slap you around at breakfast."

I thought of going into the bar for a nightcap, but nixed the idea. Then I debated about whether to buy a package of Player's Lights, but said no to that, too. I finally decided just to turn in and get a good night's sleep.

But when I opened my door, I discovered Roberta the Flack sitting on my bed.

"What," I asked her, "is the meaning of this?"

"This," she answered, "is called public relations." She wore skintight Hottie jeans, a thin T-shirt and slippers.

"I almost came back here with a friend," I told her.

She nodded. "Helene Vachon. But you didn't."

I frowned. "How do you know such things?"

Roberta smiled. "I just told you. Public relations."

She came over, wrapped her arms around my neck

and gave me the best kiss I'd had in the longest time. She pulled off her clothes, then pulled off mine. She pulled me onto the bed.

"Do you see," she whispered into my ear, "do you see what you would have missed if you had brought Helene back with you?"

"I see, I see," I said in the darkness.

12

I slept well, and, when I awoke and rolled over to give Roberta the Flack a little peck, I found no Roberta, just a note on her pillow. I read, "Glad you enjoyed your dinner and 'dessert.' Good luck with H.V."

"Thank you, Roberta," I muttered as I got out of bed. "The dinner was overpriced as hell, but your peculiar form of room service was a very nice touch. And I don't need you to wish me luck with Helene."

I showered, shaved, dressed and went downstairs to Nibbles, the coffee shop. From her seat at a window table, Dawn Baxter waved me over.

"I've already ordered you coffee," she said, pointing to the steaming white cup across from her.

I settled into a seat and took a sip. Still and hot. "Sorry I'm late." I checked her out fast. OK-looking woman, pushing forty, not trying to look younger than she was. I would have had a higher opinion of her beauty if I hadn't spent such quality time lately with cuties like Helene Vachon and Roberta the Flack.

"I am famished," I announced, looking at Dawn's English muffin. "I'm feeling that steak and scrambled eggs might work out just fine for me."

When our blond, bronze-skinned server Tanner sauntered over and fended off a yawn, I thought: Here's another Redondo Beach surfer who dreams of being a Hollywood screenwriter, or at least he wants to go back to southern California and shred the waves some more. I ordered steak and eggs, potatoes, sliced tomatoes and a large orange juice.

After Tanner went away, Dawn asked, "What, if anything, did you have for dinner last night?"

"Not nearly enough. I ate in Maureen's, the fancy place."

She laughed. "Oh, that explains why you're so hungry this morning. I hope you were able to put your Maureen's dinner on your expense account. I'll bet it was frightfully expensive."

"No, I didn't have to pay for it, and yes, it was frightfully expensive." I didn't tell her that Roberta the Flack had picked up the tab and offered herself to me as dessert. Or that she had been quite delicious.

"Are you," Dawn was asking me, "going to the Go-4-It Open in New Mexico?"

"Maybe."

Dawn nodded. "New tournament. New country club, in fact. Yolanda Rivera wants all the girl golfers to attend. Yolanda is taking the credit for creating the event, and I guess she deserves it." She paused. "We need to support our commissioner. I don't think that support has been happening enough."

"I haven't been to New Mexico very often," I told her. "But I'm sure it still has many drive-in movie theaters and trailer parks." I added, "Must be a hassle for you, eh? You live in California, but you have to go to New Mexico for the Go-4-It Open, then it's back to the Golden State for the Dinah Shore."

Dawn smirked. "I believe they call it the Kraft Nabisco now. They stopped calling it the Dinah Shore years ago."

I shrugged. "Whatever. You know what I mean. I liked Dinah Shore. She was a classy entertainer and that golf tournament was a great way to honor her memory. I think lots of people feel the way I do. If the Kraft event wasn't a big one, many players would pass on it."

"Well, I know two players who are going to be there: Winnie Baxter and Vicki Vachon."

"Dawn, let me tell you why I'm here. I want to put Vicki on the cover of *Canadian Sports* with a headline saying something like, 'The World's Next Great Woman Golfer.' What do you think of that?"

"I think," she said, "that it's a bit premature. There are other fine girls in the LPGA."

"Do you know what I see when I look at her? I see a world-class golf swing. I can tell good ones from bad ones as soon as I see them, and hers is great. Motion, grip, swing, follow-through? It's all there. Plus, she has size and strength. She must be pushing six feet tall. She can drive that ball a mile. Plus, she has the mental toughness, the tenacity, the stamina. She wants to be Numero Uno, she wants it now, and she wants it forever. The other girls just can't compete against someone like her."

Dawn smiled. "You sound just like Helene. But she's her girl's mother, right? I mean, she's *supposed* to be biased."

"Would you say that you and Helene are friends?"

Dawn laughed. "I certainly would. So would she. We're both golf others and our daughters are friends, too."

Just then I saw Roberta the Flack enter Nibbles with a large package in her arms, her dark pantsuit meticulous and immaculate. She saw me, tossed me the tiniest smile and wink—me, the man on whose cock she had come seven hours earlier—and disappeared.

"She's lovely," said Dawn of Roberta. "She does her best to make everyone happy. She gives public relations a good name."

"Yes." I smiled as my big breakfast arrived. I tried to eat and talk at the same time. I ended up eating and moaning as Dawn sipped her coffee and smirked at me.

"Too bad about Vicki's father," she said.

I swallowed. "What?"

"They're divorced, you know. I always think it's too bad when couples split up."

"Not in their case. Helene was glad to be rid of him."

Dawn lifted an eyebrow. "Alain? Ivar and I liked him. Ivar is my husband. He owns a chain of dollar stores in the Southwest, so his business keeps him on the road. He wishes he could come watch Winnie play more often."

"What's the name of your stores?"

"Buck Stop."

My mouth fell open. "You folks own *Buck Stop*? Wow."

"As I say, it keeps Ivar busy. We live in La Jolla. Life is good, most of the time."

"On the subject of Alain and Vicki Vachon, I guess if you asked them separately about their marriage and divorce, they would give you very different stories, yet both would be true. In my case, after both of my divorces, it seemed OK to blame me for everything."

She showed no interest in my marital woes. "The sad thing about Alain is that he's not there to enjoy Vicki's success, and he's so responsible for it. He taught her about golf and did far more than Helene did to foster Vicki's development as a golfer. Ivar and I sometimes remarked to each other about what a caring, selfless father Alain was."

"Hmm," I said. Then, "This isn't going to be part of my story, and I'm not sure it's even any of my damn business, but Helene said that Alain was supposed to be Vicki's manager and in fact was ripping her off. Were you aware of that?"

Dawn nodded. "Helene said that to me and I didn't believe her. What do I think happened? Well, Alain is a likable and handsome man, but he's the farthest thing from an astute money manager you'll ever find. I'm married to a very astute businessman, so I know the difference. I don't think Alain took Vicki's money to Vegas and pissed it all away. I *do* think he tried to invest it in some high-risk, high-yield things that didn't work out, and Helene made up that story about Vegas to make Alain look like the big villain."

"OK. One more thing." I swallowed another bite of breakfast. "There's this rumor going around that some ugly business went on between you and Winnie at the Cover Girl Open—"

"You mean that I burst into the locker room and slapped her around in front of Kit Manley and Lupe

Rendon?"

"Exactamundo."

She rolled her eyes. "That old story is going around, is it? It's a sad thing that some people are so bored that they have to make up stuff like that."

"So it didn't happen? They lied about it?"

"Kit Manley and Lupe Rendon were in the locker room at the end of the tournament. Winnie was beside herself with rage. She was disgusted with herself for blowing a huge lead. She was really doing great, then her game left her and she couldn't get it back. She's the type to cry out there if the ball won't drop, or her hands will start shaking so hard that a six-inch putt will seem like an overwhelming challenge. She just lost her composure and the other girls overtook her. When I went into the locker room to give her a motherly hug, I found her trying to punch out the wall. I got her into some kind of wrestling hold so she wouldn't break her hands."

"Kit Manley got freaked out enough to report the incident to the commissioner."

"That figures. That woman, if you can call her one, is just so full of anger and gender-identities that she needs to find something, or someone, to bitch about."

...

A few hours later, as Helene Vachon and I watched Vicki tee off, I told her about my talk with Dawn Baxter. Helene laughed so hard that she got the hiccups for the rest of the afternoon.

13

Whenever I run out of interesting things to write about for *Canadian Sports*—which happens more often than I would care to admit—I publish another piece asking why sports agents are allowed to live amongst us decent people. They have been here for quite a while; they're making more money than ever; and two of the most sociopathic—that is, successful—ones hung out with us in Vicki's gallery as she finished her front nine a few under par and filled her opponents with despair.

I nearly laughed at the two youngish men at the golf course, movers and shakers in dark suits, nearly falling on their Brioni-clad asses as they paced on the grass in their city-slicker shoes, mumbling important nothings into their iPhones. I would have guessed that these guys, who believed they knew how to relate to everyone and dress for every occasion, would have enough sense to show up at a golf course in khakis,

Burt "Leverage" Levenson of International Sports Management (ISM) let his briefcase dangle by his fingertips as he squawked into his cell phone. He still had a full head of mostly black hair, and he'd shaved off his mustache. With that facial hair, he'd looked too much like Elliot Gould—sneaky and sinister— and his graying sideburns made him seem softer, more human. Or at least more humane. Martin Hewitt, still looking like the Boston Celtics forward he had been for a dozen years, had proven himself a steadfast shyster for Names and Models Enterprises—NAME—for close to a decade.

If these two presumably heterosexual males had cared as much about pussy as they did money, they would have noticed that Helene Vachon's tennis-like outfit could barely block a sneeze. Her top was cut so low that I kept fearing—or praying—that her zoomers would come tumbling out.

"Nice tan," I told her. "Nice everything."

"I'll bet you say that to all the girls."

"Yeah, but this time I mean it." I wanted to add, "You are close to forty but could pass for twenty-five. Did you know that? I'll bet you did."

I wondered if soon the female golfers would start dressing like tennis players, wearing only the necessarily clothing. Tennis players dress that way out of necessity; it's physically demanding, they sweat like sows, they need lightweight, clingy duds. Also, it's fun to watch those young women—especially if they have breasts and hips and don't look too much like young men—sweating and straining out there like they're having an orgasm.

That's the ticket: Have the lady golfers dress as lady tennis players. Better still, make them play in leotards, or in their underwear. If Vicki Vachon played just in her bra and panties, I would spend the rest of my life working as her caddy for free.

I looked at her for several moments, ogling her breasts and bum, and felt pleased that she had practically already won the Hottie Classic. Leverage and Danny Hewitt competed for Helene's attention as we all walked down the fairway.

"What's with this guy?" Leverage pointed over his shoulder. "Why does he keep following us?"

"His name," Helene said, "is Clancy Wasserman. He's a writer from *Canadian Sports*. He's here to do a story on Vicki and maybe put her on the cover of his magazine."

"*Canadian Sports*?" Leverage snorted. "I can get you the top sports magazines, put Vicki on all the networks. I have them all in my pocket. I say, 'Put Vicki on,' and they say, 'Yessir!'"

"How about that, eh?" I interjected.

"Wasn't talking to you, guy—"

"My name's Clancy."

"Whichever. I was talking to Helen."

"Her name's Helene," I told him.

"Hey, Clancy," Leverage said. "Canada just called. They need you back immediately."

"Don't speak to Clancy that way," Helene said. "I'm Canadian, too. Don't say anything to him you wouldn't say to me."

"You wouldn't want to insult *her*," I said to Leverage.

"I'm just trying to do what's best for the Vachon family," Leverage said. "And the last time I checked, sportswriters didn't know much about representing star athletes."

"Bert," I said to Leverage, "no agent can say to an

athlete, 'I promise I'll get you on the cover of this magazine.' Only the bosses of the magazine can do that, and you know it. Besides, even if agents could get their clients on the covers of magazines, *you* couldn't do it because *you* just don't have enough juice."

Leverage wheeled around and faced me. "Clancy, do you know every fucking thing there is to know? Is there any field of knowledge of which you are ignorant?"

"Some wise man once said that, when it comes to agents, you should always refuse the first three offers."

"Who said that?" Leverage asked. "I'll bet you don't know. Well, I *do* know. Ben Hogan said that about a million years ago. How much did Hogan make in his entire career, and how valid are his words today? Also, Clancy, how much money do you make at your job? Not much, I'll bet, so why are you ragging on me when I try to make these Vachon ladies rich?"

"I've got a better idea," said Martin Hewitt. "Let's get her on the cover of *Vogue* or *Cosmopolitan*. We put out the rumor that *Playboy* wants her to take it off. No actual spread, of course, but just the rumor, so people will say, 'Who's Vicki Vachon and is she so hot that *Playboy* wants to do a pictorial of her?'"

"*Playboy?*" Leverage asked Martin Hewitt.

"I didn't say she would pose nude, just that *Playboy* wanted her and that would generate worldwide male interest in her," Hewitt said. "I think Vicki and glamour should become synonymous. Vicki Vachon: Sex Goddess of the LPGA. The golf world's cover girl, right? With her legs and zoomers, she makes everything look good. The endorsements never end. The phenom of ladies' golf is also staggeringly beautiful. Every woman wants to be *like* her and every man wants to be *with* her. It's a win-win situation."

Helene said, "Hello? Earth to agents calling. Guys, just remember that Vicki hasn't won the Hottie yet. Let's make sure she wins this thing before we start talking about magazine covers, endorsements and the other stuff."

Leverage shook his head. "Your girl doesn't need to win tournaments to be popular and make money, Helene. We can start making her available for endorsements right now. I have this deal memo right here. You sign it, we get busy. How's that for service?"

Helene put her hands on her hips. "She and I are heading for New Mexico next week, then it's back here to California for the Nabisco. If everything goes well at the conclusion of the Nabisco, we'll talk business with you and all the other agents offering Vicki representation. Fair enough?"

That's my girl, I thought with a smile. You tell these clowns who's boss. You let them know what's going on.

Leverage backed off. He found a comfortable place with a bit of shade and started tapping on his smartphone.

Martin Hewitt didn't move. He just diddled around with his smartphone, too.

"Gee, guys," I said, "I hope she didn't hurt your feelings."

...

Vicki Vachon impressed me as being one of the most determined golf players I had ever watched. Always aggressive, sometimes just plain cocky. That afternoon at the Hottie Classic, Vicki, with a substantial lead late in the contest, became very cautious, almost conservative—and nearly lost because of it.

Miles O'Connell, the celebrated golf-course architect from San Francisco, had poured all of his creative energies into the design of Idyllic Village's par-three seventeenth hole. In other words, he'd copied it from the twelfth at Placid Oaks, Bayporte's famous course.

Idyllic Village's seventeenth was a bit longer than Placid Oaks' twelfth, and O'Connell had installed a dumb-looking—and sometimes inoperable—waterfall at Idyllic Village instead of Placid Oaks' trees and brush.

The rest of it was the same: you ended up in the water if you hit the ball too hard or too far to the right.

That could be a big problem if you were Vicki Vachon. On your tee shot, you just basically whacked it as hard as you could, and you could whack it plenty hard.

We stood at the ropes and watched Bernice and

Vicki prepare for their tee shots. Vicki wiped her face with the towel her caddy handed her and she blew out several big breaths that made her cheeks puff out. Martin and Leverage stood by themselves, away from the rest of us, doubtless talking about other rising young stars they hadn't yet shaken down.

Vicki's mum started bitching in a low voice. "Bernice Gerard can't putt for shit—I've seen her miss a hundred easy ones. But what happens today? She sinks them all!"

"Vicki needs to make sure she doesn't end up in the water," I said. "Otherwise, she'll be fine."

Vicki's mum said, "Duh."

Bernice Gerard, a slim, swarthy woman around forty, teed off first. She always made money at these tournaments and wore what one might call very fancy sweatpants.

Bernice lifted her Titleist ball into the air, far rather than high, and it settled at the edge of the green, just missing the water. No one's idea of a great shot, certainly, but she wiped an imaginary band of sweat off her forehead and made a *Whew!* face. People laughed and clapped. Bernice did an exaggerated curtsy.

Vicki, oblivious to Bernice's solid tee shot and crowd-pleasing antics, stood over her golf bag with Brice Traynor, her caddy. They looked into the bag, over to the ball, then at each other. They whispered and nodded, shook their heads and shrugged.

She wore a sleeveless white top, blue visor and blue skirt that barely stretched over her crotch. As a dirty old man, I wondered what kind of panties she had on, and wished I could be that pair.

Vicki frowned and narrowed her eyes. The oldest-looking teenager I had ever seen.

She pulled out what appeared to be a seven-iron, went up to her tee ball and adjusted her stance.

Helene grabbed me as if I were about to run away. "Clancy!" she said through clenched teeth. "She's using a seven! That's no good! She needs something heavier!"

"She knows what she's doing," I muttered.

Vicki swung the club and, at the moment of impact, the sound of the clubface striking the ball that says, *Yeah, baby!*

Vicki's ball sailed up and out there, as if its

dimples were eyeballs looking for the flag. Tiger Woods had rarely hit a finer tee ball.

"Hole in one!" Brice called out.

"Do it! Do it!" Vicki yelled.

"Come on down!" Brice hollered as the ball started to fall.

"Grab some green!" Vicki shouted.

The ball struck the very front of the green, took a series of big bounces towards the center and rolled to within a foot or so of the cup.

Vicki pumped her fist and slapped Brice's outstretched hand.

The stamping feet of the crowd might have made the ground shake, but I paid no attention to that.

"*Baby!*" screamed the mum as she grabbed me and kissed the side of my face.

"I like *that*," I said, smirking.

"Sorry," she said, releasing me. "I get carried away."

"I hope there's more where that came from."

She ignored my remark as we watched Vicki and Brice head off to the cup.

"School's out," I said. "Time to turn in the

textbooks and piss on the teacher."

Helene laughed. "They used to say that when I was in grade school."

"The kids say that *everywhere* in Canada."

Bernice Gerard, still visibly flustered by Vicki's magnificent tee shot, composed herself enough to two-putt the hole as Vicki tapped in hers for a birdie. Going to the last hole, Vicki had a three-shot lead.

"This is an easy par five," I told Helene. "No water, no boundaries, no bullshit."

"This whole course leaves a bit to be desired," she said.

"This whole course," I said, "sucks shit. They got Miles O'Connell, a flamboyant architect from San Francisco, to come down and design it, instead of hiring someone who knows and likes golf."

Vicki stepped up, teed off, made another birdie and won the Hottie Classic by four strokes and shook the hand of Bernice Gerard, who looked as if she'd just been punched in the solar plexus.

"That was fun," I said. "Much better than being at some boring PGA tournament, watching Tiger beat the bejesus out of a bunch of professional losers."

"This was a bit more of a nail-biter, hey? Too bad for Bernice. I really think she believed she could pull this one out."

"For a moment there, she could have done it. But then Vicki got her shit together and did what she needed to do." I watched Vicki's bum bounce as she walked off towards the scorer's tent.

"I love the scenery here," I said.

14

Carver and Mo Warner's party for the winner of the Hottie Classic happened in the ballroom, but this time they had a casual event. Mo Warner dressed the way one would imagine a rich lady dressed when trying to look humble. She wore only white slacks, a cream-colored blouse, and a ring here and chain there.

Looking around, I guessed that Carver and Mo had simply invited everyone to this do. The old guys who'd attended that formal evening in their pastel suits and ridiculous patent-leather shoes now wore tan or dark sport shirts and sensible pleated slacks. Most of the golfers had already gone, the more famous ones the faster. They had gone off to other tournaments or exhibitions or other places where their names had some value. For the majority of golfers not named Vicki Vachon, this outing had been a largely unsuccessful experience. Most of the losers would go to Sussudio the following week.

Dawn and Winnie Baxter had left after Winnie, finishing something like forty-fifth, received a check for three thousand dollars. Inderjit Dhaliwal hadn't done much better, and I wondered if she was still in the States.

While Winnie got their suitcases together, Dawn Baxter hurried into the pressroom to tell me a quick goodbye.

"You'll be in Sussudio next week?" she asked.

I nodded. "Unless there's a dramatic change in plans."

She looked down at the floor. "Didn't Vicki just outdo herself this time around? Such a classy young lady. And I can't remember if she missed a single putt."

The agents had buggered off, too.

Leverage had flown off to New York City to meet with Ludwig Castellano, a linebacker who wanted to play for a team that didn't insist on urine tests.

Martin Hewitt had broomed off to the Bay Area to sign Mercedes Tappet, an Oakland high school basketball stud about the size of Shaquille O'Neal. Mercedes didn't want to play college ball; he wanted to go straight to the NBA if he and Hewitt could find a franchise that believed, as Mercedes did and Hewitt probably did not, that the overgrown kid could become the next Shaq. Hewitt probably didn't give a rat's ass what became of Mercedes, as long as Hewitt made some big, fast money off him.

Mercedes' older sisters, Bugatti and Ferrari, neither of them a pipsqueak, played basketball for Georgetown. How, and why, those two Oakland girls ended up in Washington, D.C. remained a mystery to me.

Carver already looked gooned when I went up to him at one of the bars, but he cut quite a natty figure in his blue Polo shirt, sand-colored slacks and brown loafers.

Mo stood on stage with the bandleader while her hubby and I *schmoozed*. I also ordered drinks for Vicki, Helene and myself.

An hour or so earlier, Carver and Vicki had posed for a picture, both holding up an oversized replica of the quarter-million-dollar check she had just won. The sum, chump change compared to the kind of money the men routinely pocket on tour, nevertheless represented a vast improvement over the old days of ladies' golf. The first female champs, I'm told, received pots and pans and canned food as prizes.

"That fuckin' Miles," Carver muttered into my ear. "That goddamn cocksuckin' Miles O'Connell. I paid him millions to come down here and make me a world-class course, and did you see what he built me? A course so fuckin' *easy* that some Canuck girlie-girl comes down here and she shoots *under seventy* and she's laughin' at me! There are miniature golf courses that are harder to play than mine!"

"No one is laughing at you or your golf course," I lied.

"It's a good thing Miles fuckin' O'Connell isn't here tonight. I would love to stick my driver right up his tight, pompous little ass."

Just then a younger man entered the ballroom. He had on a green jacket and dark pleated slacks. His name was Goodman Haverford, and, as the marketing director at Hottie, he'd also had the responsibility of overseeing the Hottie Classic at Idyllic Village. Trouble was, none of us had seen him until now.

"Great tournament, wouldn't you say?" Goodman asked, sipping an iced tea. "It all came off so well. I'm sure looking forward to next year. I saw many things we should all be proud of."

Carver scowled. "Name one."

Goodman shrugged. "That brand-new golf course—"

"Goodman," asked Carver, scowling even more, "have you ever *played* golf?"

Goodman shook his head. "No time for fun. I have work to do."

Without saying goodbye, I got the three drinks I'd ordered and hustled over to the table reserved for the Hottie Classic's champion. At the next table sat Roberta the Flack, making eyes at some guy and squeezing his forearm as she spoke to him. She looked at me for the briefest moment, then returned her attention to her new friend. I guessed that financially pinched Canadian sportswriters just weren't her thing.

Vicki had changed into a pair of Hottie jeans that looked painted on, frightfully expensive and irresistibly sexy. She paired these with a black crewneck sweatshirt that particularly set off her exotic duskiness. She had done all of her winner's duties, answering questions, posing for cell phone pictures, doing brief interviews with the golf cable channels, the TV stations from southern California and Arizona. Her persona was cutely modest and consistently exuberant. Who, I asked myself, would have cared about the Hottie Classic if its winner had been some plain-looking, hard-faced woman like Kit Manley or Bernice Gerard?

Vicki's mum had changed into tight, smart dark slacks and a summery yellow blouse.

I sat with them and said, "We should have invited Brice to sit with us."

"He's already gone," replied Vicki.

"Where? Why?"

"Off to the next tournament in Sussudio. On the way, he wants to do some snowboarding."

"Snowboarding," I repeated. "I guess he's got your clubs?"

Vicki nodded. "We'll meet up at the airport, then we'll all drive out to Sussudio together."

Her mum added, "Our plans have changed a bit. Vicki has accepted an offer to do a commercial in Los Angeles. A good offer. So we're going out there for that commercial, too."

"A commercial for whom?" I asked.

"For World Elite Hotels," said Helene. "The spot will feature Vicki and Hudson Gaylord other golfers, and some other guy, a comic..."

"Shit, Mum!" Vicki rolled her eyes. "He's Buddy Sperling, and he's had his own show for years. He plays in the major PGAs." She added, "The other two golfers? They're Troy Frisby and Teddy Crossley. Both Canadians, just like us. If that makes any difference. I think that World Elite, despite its name, is a very American hotel chain."

"Did some agent set this up during the Hottie Classic?" I wanted to know.

Helene shook her head. "No agents. The director of the commercial emailed us and ran it down for us, and we said yes."

"Hudson Gaylord," I told them, "is a crucial part

of the PGA Tour. He says the dumbest, most offensive things. He gets drunk. He belches and says, 'There's a kiss for you.'"

"The director of the commercial said in his email, 'I saw Vicki on TV and knew I had to put her in my commercial.' He offered us a certain amount; I wanted double, and he said fine." Helene paused. "Say, why don't you join us for this? The three of us can fly out there, and I'll email the director to book a room for you. Maybe you'll get some good material for your story. How about it?"

I nodded, and Vicki pointed at the stage. "Clancy! They want you up there! The bandleader just introduced you as 'the famous sportswriter from Canada'! You have to go say hi."

With everyone in the ballroom staring at and applauding me, I got up, skulked over to the stage, went up the steps and stood at the microphone. I said the pap that most gracious speakers say.

"Congratulations, Vicki! Great tournament! Fine job done by all to make this such a success!" Then I told them the only golf joke I knew: "Golfers swing a stiff shaft."

I heard Carver's unmistakable cackle as I left the stage.

Back at the winner's table, I said to Helene, "Get me that room. I'm going to that commercial shoot with you and Vicki."

"Done," she said with a smile.

Mo Warner got up and sang for much of the evening. When she finally stopped, everyone applauded for the longest time. I couldn't be sure if people clapped because they'd enjoyed her singing or they were grateful that she'd finally stopped.

On my way out, I shook Carver's hard and thanked him for his hospitality. "Don't worry about your golf course. It's just a few months and a few million dollars from being adequate. Just don't let Miles O'Connell anywhere near it."

He laughed and pumped my hand. "Golfers swing stiff shafts," was all he said.

PART TWO

YOU SEXY THING

15

I would never have guessed that it takes billions of dollars and thousands of people to shoot one TV commercial. I had no clue how many doughnuts and urns of coffee those people would consume, either.

I'm exaggerating, of course. Maybe a couple hundred people made the commercial. The cables, wires and other pieces of equipment vastly outnumbered the workers, although one could be forgiven for thinking that this commercial was some sort of Hollywood big deal. They shot the spot at an actual World Elite Hotel in Century City; the cables and wires snaked throughout the hotel's lobby to a trailer parked outside, and everyone rushed about with the urgency one normally associates with emergency rooms receiving the victims of ten-car collisions.

Bright Ideas, the advertising agency making the commercial, wanted to remind all golfers, all cute people and all cute golfers that World Elite Hotels were great places to stay. Bright Ideas, founded by Richard Bright, had moved from Manhattan to Vernon, New Jersey after Bright and his New York landlord had a conflict over some practical matters, such as how much the agency's rent should be. Alas, Bright, a fitness fanatic, dropped dead in the middle of a pick-up basketball game at the nearby YMCA. Yadranka, Bright's widow, now owned the agency, but scarcely knew how to contact it and let the "peons" run it. She spent most of her time in Miami, with her TV and three poodles.

Most of what I learned from that experience came from Kai, the director, and Alix, his assistant.

Kai, in his mid-thirties, had a full head of graying black hair and quite badly needed a shave. His Levi's and runners had many little tears and holes. He wore a gray sweatshirt emblazoned with the message:

AND I WENT TO USC FILM SCHOOL FOR *THIS?*

Alix, a passably pretty woman in her late twenties, wore tattered jeans, a sweat-stained T-shirt and a Los

Angeles Dodgers baseball cap. I had a hunch she'd been one of Kai's classmates and disliked her job as much as he did his. Around her waist, on a toolbelt, she had a dozen cell phones and radios. Many wires and cords hung from her body.

Alix walked fast, chewed bubblegum and fidgeted with her equipment; her colleagues, especially the males, jumped out of her way.

As Alix hurried past, I heard one male crew member mutter, "Keep going, bitch. That's right. Nobody's home."

Just then, we all heard Alix shout into a cell phone, "Where are you, Lance? Where the fuck *are* you? Get your *ass* over here or you won't have a fucking job! Hear me, *Lance*?"

...

The sponsors of the Hottie Classic had kindly provided limousine service for the Vachons to get from Idyllic Village to the World Elite Hotel in Century City.

I had a rental car. I drove to Palm Springs for lunch, then headed down to Los Angeles, where I returned my car and got a taxi to Century City, which is not a city but just another neighborhood in Los Angeles. To me, Century City is a blah place, and the World Elite Hotel is just a bit better than Holiday Inn. I would much rather have stayed in Hermosa Beach or Malibu. I wondered if the waves were good, and if so, whether the surfers were out there, punching each other in the nose over who got to go first.

The Vachons couldn't have dinner with me. They got room service instead and Vicki fretted over what to wear for the commercial. She also worried about starting work at six in the morning.

I spent that evening in the lobby bar, listening as other people *kvetched*.

An interior decorator or designer bitched about his impossible-to-please Hong Kong clients who'd just moved to Pacific Palisades. A surgical-instruments salesman moaned about his client, an asshole doctor in Bel Air.

Not long after, a blonde cutie sat down next to me at the bar. She looked barely old enough to drink and said she was in "the entertainment business."

She leaned over and said, "For five hundred

dollars, I'll go to your room with you and we'll do whatever you like. For a thousand, I'll stay the night."

"I'd love it," I told her. "But the doctor still has me on meds from the last time I went to the Mustang Ranch."

She made a bit of a face and moved on to the next mark, but I knew our little exchange was nothing compared to what Phil Ruble said years ago back in Bayporte.

Phil, still one of the new guys at *Canadian Sports*, had covered a game in Calgary between the Northup Kodiaks and Calgary Dinosaurs. After the game, he wanted to return to his hotel room and work on his report. He and a few other reporters were in the elevator when a comely Calgarian stepped inside and said, "For three hundred dollars, I will go to your room and do anything." She looked at them all. *"Anything."*

Phil spoke up. "How fast can you type?"

...

The only person who failed to show up for the shoot at six in the morning was Hudson Gaylord, the *shmuck* of the PGA Tour. But people mostly just sat around while the makeup and wardrobe specialists prettied up the actors. The bosses kept ordering the camera and lighting people to move the equipment here, then there, then back again. Those with nothing to move drank coffee, munched on doughnuts and smiled because they were on the clock, didn't have to get off their asses yet and presumably got their coffee and doughnuts for free.

The hotel had provided a "green room" for the actors and their hangers-on to relax and stuff themselves with refreshments between takes. The boardroom served as the "set," and Alix had one of her crew members escort the actors from the greenroom to the set and back again, and to make sure that they didn't run out of goodies in the greenroom. The actors could watch a TV set that showed the activity on the set, and they could hear what the crew members were saying.

Helene and I sat in the green room and read some news sites on our iPads while Vicki sat in the makeup room. Helene went in a few times to see how her girl looked.

"They're turning her into Kim Basinger," Helene

said. "She looks magnificent."

"Runs in the family," I said.

"Coming on to me again, eh?"

"No, just stating a fact."

Just then Buddy Sperling entered the green room and helped himself to a doughnut and coffee. He had that celebrity's habit of walking into a room and forgetting that other people were already in there.

Buddy—stoop-shouldered, flabby waisted and gray-haired—came in wearing an aloha shirt, khaki shorts and sandals. He had a cell phone pressed to his ear and smiled like a man who knew he would get laid that evening. He sat next to us but threw one leg over the other and faced the wall.

He starred in *Buddy's Here*, a TV series in which he played a ruthless Los Angeles businessman who retires, puts on filthy clothes and moves into skid row, where he tries to help the downtrodden rebuild their lives. Much of the show's humor came from his attempts at assisting people who merely wished for him to fuck off. The show, frequently tasteless and highly offensive to black, gay and mentally ill people, had become a colossal hit.

Yippee Mendelson came into the green room. He, too, had accepted a part in the commercial. A member of the PGA Senior Tour, he had just come from the makeup room, where the specialist had done her best to cover up the scars of alcoholic desolation on Yippee's face. His stiff, stringy hair, difficult not to stare at, presented another challenge. So did his posture, which was even worse than Buddy's.

Yippee introduced us to his brother, who looked at us as if he were a lifelong movie buff who'd just arrived backstage at the Oscars.

"This is Sherman," said Yippee. "He served in Vietnam. He idolizes golfers. Isn't that so, Sherm?"

Sherman nodded.

"Thank you for your service in Vietnam," I said. "You military guys are America's heroes."

He shook his head. "Was nothing. Golfers are the heroes."

"Golfers are just entertainers. Soldiers are the defenders of liberty."

"No, sir, you got it wrong," he said.

I shrugged. I hated to argue; even more, I hated anyone who couldn't accept a compliment.

"I'll tell you the name of a true American hero," said Sherman. "Hudson Gaylord."

"Hey?"

Sherman nodded. "You heard me. My brother took me to a tournament where I got to see all these great golfers. I felt like I died and went to heaven. Afterwards, we went to this restaurant, and do you know who was there?"

"Hudson Gaylord?" I asked.

"Yes! Before he left, do you know what Hudson did?"

I smiled. "I'll bet he came over and said hi to you and your brother."

"Oh, he did more than that. Hudson Gaylord shook my hand." Sherman stared at the shaken hand for a moment and fought back tears. "That wonderful man, who surely had better things to do, came by and shook my hand. I'll never forget that moment."

"Pretty heavy stuff," I said.

At close to nine, Alix entered the green room, did a visual sweep of the premises, then exited. She said into her radio, "*Hudson Gaylord has arrived. He is on the premises."*

I could hear her as she marched down the hallway, saying the same thing.

"Hudson Gaylord," I said to Helene. "What a douche bag."

"He can't be as bad as all that."

"No? Just wait till you meet him." I looked at my iPad and started reading the *Los Angeles Tribune* story about the Hollywood movie producer and his wife who, in an effort to stimulate the economy, terminated two of their illegals and replaced them with carded domestic workers.

16

That pro golfer and American *mensch* Hudson Gaylord entered the green room bitching at Sol Lowenthal, his agent, the hugely respected principal at Creative Sports Management—CSM—and a man known for his refusal to tolerate abusive clients. But Sol tolerated Hudson, mainly because, for reasons Sol himself certainly found puzzling, Hudson had remained an entertaining public figure who made big money for CSM.

"Sol, do you remember what I asked for?" Hudson asked, looking as red-faced and petulant as a little kid who'd just been denied dessert. "I wanted a stretch limo, and what did you send me? A fucking Hummer! Do you know what Hummers do to my hemorrhoids? And I asked for a basket of mixed fruit. You got me a basket of bananas! Do I look like a fucking chimp? And how about the bottles of *ice water*? Those bottles were lukewarm! I can't drink lukewarm water in the California heat! I wanted a suite, but you got me a room. I wanted a TV in the shitter, but no TV. Sol, what do you do for me? I know what *I* do for *you*: I stand there like an asshole while you shake me down for your commission. On the tour, they say, 'You got to get yourself a kike. Everyone has one. You need yours. They run the world.' So I go get mine, but what's he good for? He can't help me with my putts, he can't get me my limo, he can't come through with the mixed fruit or ice water. He can't even make sure there's a TV in the shitter. Tell me, Sol, what do you do for me?"

Hudson looked down at the snacks arrayed on the table. "This is for me, right?" His question was rhetorical; he did not want an answer.

He picked up an apple, bit into it and chewed with his mouth wide open.

"Sol," he continued, "you could have done better for me on this gig. You could have gotten me twice what you settled for. They would have come through with the number if you had held out. You said, 'Hudson, you're being paid twice as much as the other people on this project. Makes you happy, yes?' But

Solly, there's nobody else on this project who's worth half as much as Hudson Gaylord! Do you know who Hudson Gaylord is? The rest of the world sure as fuck does. Maybe you've forgotten. Time to wake up and remember who your best clients are."

I sat there and smiled, as I always did when people referred to themselves in the third person. With celebrities, I found it that much more amusing.

Sol nodded and provided whichever facial expression Hudson seemed to want—a smile, pout or frown—but I had to believe that the agent had heard so much whining from his client for so long that Sol took little of it seriously.

Half a dozen years earlier, Hudson Gaylord had come on the golf scene, a strapping, handsome man, just out of college, with some prestigious amateur titles to boast of. And he *did* boast. He could play golf far better than many men a decade or more older. Unfortunately, he also became known as the PGA's most insufferable prick.

Even the most naïve dingbats found him impossible to like, but because of Hudson's good looks and masterful golfing ability, they gave him good press.

If Hudson disliked me, he had good reason to do so. I loathed him and, in my own sneaky way, went after him in print. Whenever I covered a golf event that he won, I mentioned him as the champion, then ignored him and wrote about the other players.

But Hudson, who may have been illiterate and clearly was unaware of how I had mistreated him in print, perhaps did not even know my occupation and why he kept encountering me on golf courses and at golf-related events.

He saw me there in the green room, sitting next to Helene. He checked her out, for she looked hot, then, probably because she obviously was just another cutie and not a celebrity, he dismissed her and looked at me some more.

"I've seen you before," he said to me.

"Same here," I replied. "But I've forgotten your name."

Sol grinned and said, "What's up, Clancy?"

"I'm here doing a story on Vicki Vachon. This is her mother, Helene."

Sol shook her hand. "We've talked on the phone.

Did you like what I offered?"

Helene shrugged. "Still thinking about it."

Sol said, "Hudson, you know Clancy Wasserman, the sportswriter from Canada. He writes for *CS*."

"Golf writer from Canada," Hudson said with a bit of a sneer.

"Oh? Have you read me?" I retorted. "Did you have much trouble with the big words?"

Helene stared at Hudson with disgust and fascination, the way people do when driving past gory car crashes.

"Did you say," she asked Hudson, "that you're getting twice as much money for this commercial as my daughter?"

"Who's your daughter?" he asked.

"Vicki Vachon."

"Who the fuck is Vicki Vachon?"

"She's on the LPGA Tour," Helene said, her face hardening.

Hudson gave her a big smile. "Wow! Vicki Vachon from the LPGA Tour! Can I have her autograph?"

Helene shook her head. "I can't believe you're getting twice what she's getting."

"That's called capitalism," Hudson told her. "You get what you're worth."

I leaned over towards Hudson and said, "Don't be such an asshole."

He snarled at me. "Who the fuck asked *you*?"

Sol took Hudson by the arm and led him to a corner for a two-man huddle. Yippee and Sherman gobbled up snacks and Buddy Sperling pocketed his cell phone and looked around the room.

We all felt startled when Buddy Sperling, veteran comic and, for the time being, major TV star, rushed to the doorway and said, "Please marry me! Oh, please! Please!"

Vicki Vachon stood before him, striking a cheesecake pose, a hand on her hip, a smile on her made-up face. Black hair flowing past her shoulders, minidress showing plenty of smooth, tanned skin. Breasts plump and firm, tummy tight, legs going on forever. Tee & A.

Hey, if you got it, flaunt it.

17

"Places, everyone!" Kai called out, even though everyone was already in place, and the performers already started to look bored.

From the green room, we watched the goings on. Helene, Sol, Sherman and this or that crew member who popped in to grab a handful of food.

Kai fretted over his four performers the way I imagined Scorsese or Tarantino fretted over the placement of everyone and everything. Vicki and Hudson sat next to each other at a table; across from them were Yippee and Buddy.

Kai had placed props—coffee mugs, pens and notebooks—in front of the performers, and kept moving those items around before returning them to their original positions.

We watched guys in the corners with cameras on their shoulders as they took turns panning the room. They moved about like square dancers—allemande left, dosado—and zoomed in and out.

"Why are they goofing around like that?" Helene asked me.

"They're not just 'goofing around,' they're professionals who are figuring out what they need to do."

She and I burst out laughing. Sol smiled. Sherman glowered at us.

Just then we heard, but could not see, Kai.

"Buddy has the first line. He will simply ask the question I feed him. You guys talk as we record it. our goal is to get two fifteen-second spots and three thirty-second ones from all this chaos. The one thing you people have in common is golf. The whole purpose of this project is to get the four of you to send out the message, 'Hey! People who like golf and have lots of money! World Elite is the place to stay!' But make damn sure you keep your answers brief. One word, if possible, because in advertising, one word can often say more than an entire sentence. I hope we don't have any garrulous types here today."

"One more thing," said Alix. "Have fun, take it easy, let us do the work. Feel free to get something to eat or drink. Take a bathroom break if nature calls. Doesn't matter if you sneeze, cough, fart or belch. If your undies are a problem, stand up and adjust your junk. No one will be offended."

Hudson asked, "What's this about fifteen and thirty seconds?"

"We're making commercials that run fifteen and thirty seconds," Kai said.

"Fifteen seconds," said Yippee, "is not enough time for a commercial."

"Our job," said Kai, "is to make sure that fifteen seconds is more than enough."

Alix appeared on our screen. "Buddy," she said, "please stop looking at Vicki like you're at a peep show."

Buddy Sperling immediately shifted his eyes from Vicki's breasts. "Can't help it. Haven't seen melons like hers in ages."

Helene rolled her eyes at me.

I shrugged. "Vicki doesn't seem to be embarrassed about it."

"She's used to be ogled."

Vicki said, "Do you want me to put on something

else?"

"No," said Kai. "You're fine just as you are."

"Fuckin'-A," said Buddy.

"Let's do this thing," Hudson said. "I have a flight this afternoon, and I'm going to be on it even if this isn't done."

Alix shouted, "OK! Ready to roll!"

"No!" Vicki cried out, making an awful face and turning her head away from Hudson. "I need to sit somewhere else."

Hudson stuck his hand up in the air like a basketball player who'd just fouled his opponent. "My bad. I admit it. You said it was OK to fart."

Buddy Sperling stood up and said, "Come over here, Vicki. I'll sit next to him. I won't let his unholy flatulence get to me. I'll just breathe through my mouth."

Vicki gave Buddy a big, grateful smile as he pulled out the chair, she rose and he sat where she had been.

"I consider it an honor," Buddy said, "to sit next to Hudson Gaylord, even if the area reeks of bowel gas."

Then the screen went blank. Helene got up and

said, "This is all too weird for me. I need a cigarette. OK if I smoke in here? If not, say so and I'll step outside."

"Stay here and smoke," I told her.

"Yeah, stay put," said Sol.

Sherman shrugged.

Helene lit up exhaled. "Clancy," she said, "isn't Hudson Gaylord just the most obnoxious cunt alive?"

I nodded. "He's one of them. I've met others."

She looked at Sol Lowenthal. "How can you stand him? He carried on like a spoiled child. Does he really make you *that* much money?"

Sol paused. "There must be something I like about him, even if I'm reluctant to admit it. I could fire him tomorrow, just as he could fire me. But we keep working together because, in some perverse way, we admire each other."

"Besides," I said, "it's all part of an act. Hudson Gaylord is the man we love to hate and hate to love. In private, he probably chills out and is not so bad."

Helene stood there staring at me.

"I've heard the same about Charles Manson. He has his moments when he's an OK enough guy despite his public image."

Helene and Sol stared at me.

"What?" I asked, looking from one to the other. "I'm just telling you what I've heard."

Sol turned to Helene. "After admiring Vicki this morning, I want to triple every number I've bandied about concerning her earning potential."

Helene nodded. "Thank you, Sol. But she and I aren't going to make any agency commitments until after the Nabisco Open."

. . .

In spite of themselves, Kai and his hooligans got some work done that morning. Much of the footage they shot looked crisp and tight, and was the kind of stuff one might want to upload on YouTube and laugh about, but I questioned its value as material they could shape into fifteen- or thirty-second spots.

Here is a sample:

BUDDY: Yippee, what's your favorite golf course?
YIPPEE: Arabella, South Africa.
HUDSON: Pebble Beach.

BUDDY: Hudson, why Pebble Beach?

HUDSON: Because I beat everyone's ass there.

YIPPEE: Pebble Beach is a great course?

HUDSON: I'll change my answer to Saint Edwards or Saint Andrews—whatever the fuck it's called. In Scotland.

YIPPEE: Saint Andrews. Did you win there?

HUDSON: Maybe. What's it to ya?

BUDDY: Vicki, which is *your* favorite?

VICKI: Placid Oaks, up in Canada.

HUDSON: Placid Oaks? In Bayporte? Shit.

VICKI: I'll pretend I didn't hear that.

KAI: Guys, let's keep it clean and try to say stuff that will make people want to stay at World Elite Hotels. Back to you, Buddy.

BUDDY: OK, next question: What's your favorite golf club? Mine is my driver. Actually, it isn't, but this is a family commercial, so I'll say driver.

YIPPEE: Mine is my five-iron. You see—

BUDDY: Hudson?

HUDSON: Favorite club? Who cares?

BUDDY: It's Kai's idea. Be a sport.

HUDSON: Six-iron, then.

BUDDY: Vicki?

VICKI: My putter.

BUDDY: You're playing golf naked—

HUDSON: Naked? What kind of retard does that?

BUDDY: Bear with me.

VICKI: No pun intended.

BUDDY: Everyone, shut up. You're playing naked; do you wear shoes or gloves?

HUDSON: I won't answer. The question is too stupid.

BUDDY: I'll answer: I would wear shoes. If I'm naked, I would need to keep one hand free to manipulate the club God gave me.

VICKI: HAHAHAHA!

KAI: Take five, people.

18

As a moderately popular Canadian writer, I occasionally receive invitations—or at least suggestions—to write about things other than sports. Showbiz, for example. Alas, my only entertainment-industry thoughts are that Eddie Murphy and Jim Carrey have made pretty much the same movies for the past two decades, and at times I've wished that Osama had taken out Hollywood instead of the Twin Towers. But I did have some feedback for Vicki as she, her mum and I sat in the green room, all of us speaking scarcely above a whisper as Vicki gobbled up some fresh fruit.

"Vicki," I said, "you can take over this project and use it to promote yourself. It really is yours. Just snatch it away from those clowns and say, 'I'll take it from here.'"

"Can you *believe* Hudson Gaylord?" she asked, swallowing a mouthful of banana. "He's vulgar. He farts and laughs about it. He's a great golfer, but..." She closed her eyes and shuddered.

Helene said, "We'll put it into her contract: 'No working with Hudson Gaylord, or anyone else like him, under any circumstances.'"

I nodded. "He can eat, drink, sleep, piss and shit. He can also play golf very well most of the time. He's not much good for anything else."

Vicki shrugged. "I don't really have much more to say about him."

"Oh, but you *do*," I told her. "You have plenty to say in this commercial. Look, have you ever gone into a tournament and ended up playing a certain kind of shot for the first time? I mean, it's a new course to you and you're trying new things? Improvising, innovating?"

She narrowed her eyes. "I try not to do that. I stick to what's worked for me."

I smiled. "Good. If you can fit that in somewhere in this commercial, do it. Try, 'I don't know how to answer that question, because in a tournament, I don't like trying new things.' You see what I mean? Kai will go for that. He'll see that you're giving the viewer a personal insight into yourself. You're also giving your audience a golf tip. That's what Kai wants.

He'll include that in the final version of the commercial that actually goes on the air."

"I hope you're paying attention," Helene said to her daughter.

"I am, I am." For the very first time, I saw the hardness of annoyance on Vicki's face when she looked at her mother.

"Here's something I guarantee they're going to ask you: 'What's the most difficult shot to make?' What will you say?"

Vicki chuckled. "They're *all* difficult."

"Wrong answer. You pick out something you find particularly hard, and you talk about it. Got that?"

Vicki frowned. "The problem *I* have is getting too cocky out there, and I get sloppy. Sometimes I just have to get back to fundamentals and play solid golf."

I snapped my fingers. "Yes! Say that! I'm sure you have a hundred more tips from the golf academy and other places. We know that golf is mostly mental once you learn to swing the clubs, but a zillion people out there refuse to believe that, and they'll love to hear whatever you have to say."

"Are you taking this all in?" Helene asked Vicki.

Vicki rolled her eyes. *"Mum…"*

Here is what happened later on:

KAI: We're doing great, people. I can really feel this coming together.

ALIX: We're rolling. Everyone who's not supposed to be talking, shut the fuck up!

KAI: Do it, Buddy.

BUDDY: All right, folks. If you could play any course in the world tomorrow, which one would it be?

YIPPEE: Diamond Country Club in Vienna.

HUDSON: Diamond? Come the fuck on, man.

YIPPEE: I'm serious. Diamond is great.

HUDSON: So is my ass.

BUDDY: I've never actually played at Parkstone, but I've read great things about it. So that's what I'll say.

HUDSON: Parkstone isn't jackshit.

VICKI: You're such a classy guy, Hudson.

HUDSON: What? I'm just being honest.

VICKI: I'm going to cheat a bit and say any course in Hawaii. I just *love* that whole group of islands.

HUDSON: Hawaiian courses are no better than the others.

VICKI: Why don't *you* name one, then?

HUDSON: Like I just said, they all blow lunch. You'll feel that way soon enough, too, girlie.

VICKI: I seriously doubt that.

HUDSON: *Do* you? *I* think you'll be burned out before you get your cherry popped.

VICKI: OK…

BUDDY: Next question: What's your hardest golf shot, Yippee?

YIPPEE: The first one, the tee shot. If that goes well, I can manage the rest of it OK.

BUDDY: How about you, Hudson?

HUDSON: Ask me something else. There are no hard shots, just bad golfers.

VICKI: Surprise!

HUDSON: What's *that* supposed to mean, girlie?

VICKI: Just what I said.

BUDDY: Vicki, what's the toughest shot for you?

VICKI: The last putt of the last round, when I know my hot boyfriend is waiting for me with a cold drink.

KAI: Bravo! Terrific, Vicki! Say it again, but as you

say it, get up and walk over to the refrigerator and get a pop. But leave out hot boyfriend and cold drink.

VICKI: The last putt of the last round, when my boyfriend is waiting for me.

KAI: Terrific! Next question, Buddy.

BUDDY: What is the one thing you need in order to become a champion golfer? Besides being named Tiger Woods.

HUDSON: Woods has a bad left knee. He ends up in bunkers and trees, too.

YIPPEE: Have you looked at Woods' stats? All those majors he's won? The guy is not quite human.

HUDSON: He wins some and loses some, just like everyone else. His competition is usually a bunch of bozos, anyway.

YIPPEE: Hudson, could you possibly be any dumber?

HUDSON: I could buy and sell you twenty times over, pal.

BUDDY: Let's move on. How does a person become a champ? Hudson?

HUDSON: Be good at what you do and get lucky. Not a whole lot more to it than that.

KAI: Same question to Vicki.

BUDDY: Well, Vicki?

VICKI: Everyone says, "I want to win." That's an easy thing to say. But if you look closely, you'll find that some of those people show up, do the best they can and seem happy enough if they win a few bucks. But the people who win, really *win*, are those who say, "I refuse to lose. Losing is for losers. I would rather die than lose." At least, that's my two cents.

KAI: Cut! That's a wrap! Yea!

19

Way up there above the town of Sussudio, in a region far too rugged ever to attract many people, sat the Mescaline Country Club and Resort. It wasn't really named Mescaline any more than the town was Sussudio. I have always had difficulty with Native names, which is odd, since I'm from Canada, a country filled with Native place names.

When I arrived at the resort, I turned in my rental car to a young parking attendant who looked and acted as if he would rather be skiing. Then I met Can't Swim and Always Stoned.

The parking attendant told me that Can't Swim and Always Stoned were the resort's two Native bosses. Can't Swim and Always Stoned stood beaming at the resort's main entrance. They had appointed themselves the welcoming committee to new arrivals, and I was one of them.

Can't Swim and Always Stoned looked like a

couple of stock characters from Hollywood. Can't Swim wore a herringbone three-piece suit, a Washington Redskins T-shirt, a Castrol Oil cap and tattered Nikes. Always Stoned wore a Cleveland Indians jersey, cargo pants and a Peterbilt cap.

A huge banner flapped a bit as it hung from the lodge's roof. The banner read:

WELCOME TO THE
GO-4-IT ENERGY DRINK GOLF CLASSIC

"We have many women who come here to play golf," said Can't Swim as he shook my hand. "Women love to gamble, too. Play slots, lose money. Good stuff."

"Hey! Nice to meet you!" said Always Stoned as we shook hands. "You like to gamble, too, right? Play poker, shoot craps?"

"Sorry to disappoint you," I said. "I'm a sportswriter from Canada. I'm here to write about the golf tournament."

"So you'll write good things about us," said Can't Swim, "and people will come from all over to visit us and leave their money?"

I nodded. "I will write about the women who come here to golf and gamble."

They both smiled. Perhaps they were happy to have a professional writer on the premises who could provide them with plenty of free publicity.

"You see the lodge here?" asked Can't Swim. "It's only a few stories tall, but big enough. See the brown building that looks like a big cookie? That's our casino. A walkway connects the bedrooms to the casino. It's as comfy as you can get."

Sections of the Mescaline Country Club were visible from the roadway leading up to the resort. I saw greens and tees that all looked to be in imminent danger of tumbling over and falling off the plateau.

Helene and Vicki were supposed to be right behind me. Our deal was to fly from Los Angeles to Texas and then Brice Traynor would drive them and I would drive myself.

"So, where the fuck is Brice?" I asked Helene.

She shrugged. "The hotel in New Mexico said he'd

checked out, but he's not answering his cell phone."

"I'll wait here with you," I said. "If he doesn't show up, we'll just all drive out there together."

"He has my golf clubs," Vicki said.

"When did you last speak to him?" I asked.

"A couple of days ago," said Helene.

"Maybe it's car trouble," I said.

"I don't care what's going on," Vicki said. "Just so long as I'm reunited with my clubs."

Helene said, "You just go on ahead, Clancy. We'll wait here for another hour, and if he doesn't turn up, we'll just get a rental car. It's really not very far."

Vicki harrumphed. "I'm going to this thing with almost no practice, no clubs and maybe no caddy. What a pisser!"

Brice Traynor didn't materialize, but Helene and Vicki didn't have to rent a car. The resort's courtesy shuttle arrived and the ladies boarded. The driver's name must have been Goes Too Fast.

As the shuttle pulled up to the resort's front gate, Helene and Vicki fairly shook from exhaustion, anxiety and Goes Too Fast's driving.

"We made it, Clancy." Helene telephoned me in my room. "We're going to have a room-service dinner and spend the rest of the evening trying to locate Brice."

"Good luck with that," I told her.

The next day, at about noon, Helene called my room again. "Nada. I've called the New Mexico cops and told them that a friend hadn't arrived and may be in trouble somewhere between Texas and New Mexico."

"I'll stop by your room in a few minutes," I said, "and take Vicki over to the pro shop here so that she can get some replacement clubs."

"Oh, she'll *love* that. Like she's not crabby enough right now over Brice's disappearance."

Vicki, as promised, was hotter than July when we entered the Mescaline Resort's pro shop and met Huey Clegg, the manager or head pro or something. Thirtyish and shaggy haired, he handed us his business card, which read ATHLETIC DIRECTOR. Over in a corner, Huey's assistant, a teenager named Kirk, dozed as he sat on a stool.

Although we did not ask, Huey told us a bit about himself. He had worked at golf courses I had never heard of throughout Texas and New Mexico. He had been a caddy, assistant pro and, now, head pro.

"This place?" he said. "It's pretty new. They built the casino first, of course. The casino provided the money for the hotel, and the casino and hotel provided the money for the golf course. And this resort as a whole attracts people to buy the homes nearby. Of course, this resort is sitting on Native land, and you can't build private houses on Native land.

"The course looks challenging, but it really isn't. if you stand on a tee like the fifteenth, you may think, 'Whoa! I'm having to hit the ball straight as an arrow or it'll end up in the sand trap.' But that's not the case. Make a decent drive and you'll be on the green."

Vicki nodded. "I can drive the ball pretty straight."

"Then you should be OK," Huey said.

"Who designed this thing?" I asked.

"Candy Ass," he replied.

"Never heard of him," I said.

"Miles O'Connell designed it. Can't Swim named him Candy Ass when O'Connell came out here while the course was still only partway done. They were at the first tee when it started to rain. O'Connell freaked out: 'Oh, my God! My lovely jacket! It'll get ruined!' He was wearing this fancy bomber jacket made of the most expensive leather, and he was terrified that it would get wet. So he goes running everywhere, looking for shade, but of course no shade had been built yet. But the rain just stopped as fast as it started, and he started sobbing and checking out his jacket for spots on rain. We all thought it was funny, this man carrying on about a piece of clothing."

As Vicki started picking through items in the pro shop, Huey trailed her, his eyes glued to her bum.

"Vicki," I asked, "which concerns you more, Brice or your clubs?"

"Brice can look after himself," she replied. "I'm sure he's OK. I want my clubs back. I know them and they know me."

She found what she wanted, or at least would settle for—Titleist, Ping and Taylormade woods and irons.

"You can borrow them for the tournament," said Huey. "No charge. If you decide you want to buy them, we'll figure out the price before you leave."

Vicki smiled. "Good. Now, where would I find a caddy?"

"You're looking at him," Huey said.

"Really?"

He nodded. "I'll expect twenty percent of your winnings," he said. "First prize is three hundred thousand dollars. If you win, that means sixty thousand for me."

"And you'll deserve every dime of it. But who will mind the shop?"

Huey pointed at Kirk. "He can manage the place as well as I can. It needs no managing because it does no business. Most of the golfers here have their clubs custom made somewhere else and wouldn't condescend to buy anything from us. They're also really bad golfers."

"Do you mean it?" Vicki asked, wide-eyed. "About being my caddy?"

"I mean it."

"You rock, dude!" She raised her hand, and he

slapped it.

"Do you want to play a practice round today?"

She nodded.

"Then meet me at the course in an hour. I'll get your equipment together and put it all in a top-quality bag. Twenty balls OK?"

Vicki smiled. "Fine."

"Vicki," I said, "we still don't know anything about Brice. Aren't you worried?"

"Brice is OK."

"Do you know something I don't?"

She shrugged. "Kinda."

"Then spill it."

"He's met someone else. She's as slutty as he is. And he is *so* fired."

Instead of serving up one of my usual wisecracks, I said, "Too bad, eh? Brice was a good caddy."

Vicki shook her head. "He didn't choose my clubs or help me read the greens. He just carried my shit. I can get along without him. All I really want is someone who will wipe off my clubs and keep his mouth shut unless I ask him something."

"How do you know he hasn't been in an

accident?"

She made a face. "Like what? He fucked her too hard and sprained his cock?"

20

Brice Traynor called Helene and Vicki the night before the tournament and explained himself.

"He says he's found himself and has never been so happy," Vicki told me over dinner at the Tee Pee Room. "He's in love with some chick and he says he's sorry about the car trouble he had. Then he apologized for the bad weather he encountered. He said we would love Glynnis if we ever met her." She paused, sneering. "I didn't know there was anyone named Glynnis."

I nodded. "The other woman is usually named Tawny."

"Brice sounded breathless over the phone," Vicki went on. "He said that nothing in his life had ever prepared him for what he experienced the moment he walked into Joe's Good Grub and met Glynnis, the server who brought him his enchiladas and margaritas. They went snowboarding as soon as she got off work and were married last night.

"They exchanged vows at the foot of one of the runs, and Brice's longtime pal Roach O'Reilly married them. He said that Roach had been ordained by the legendary Ram Dass, a former Harvard professor."

"How about that, eh?" I said.

"Brice now knows that he has begun a long, enlightening trip with Glynnis. He is sorry that some poor, misguided soul broke into his car and stole my golf clubs, but he says that I must try to overcome desires and attachments to such trivial things because desires and attachments prevent me from reaching nirvana. He believes he has some pay coming and wants me to mail him a check at his new address." She frowned. "Like he doesn't think he owes *me* any money for *my* golf clubs that were in *his* possession when someone ripped them off."

"Brice really thinks he's on some road to enlightenment?" I shook my head. "I wonder what kind of cigarettes *he's* been smoking."

A bit later, we hung out in the casino. I lost a couple of hundred dollars at the blackjack table, while Helene chain-smoked Player's Lights and plunked a hundred dollars' worth of silver tokens into the slot machines.

After that, we three wandered into the resort's shopping arcade. Vicki and Helene smiled and nodded at the other women who'd come to compete in the tournament. In the stores, we gazed at many Native beaded dresses and western hats.

"Where are the bullfight posters?" I asked Helene. "I don't even see any velvet portraits of Elvis."

"We'll take you downtown tomorrow," she said. "Maybe there are art galleries and shops where you can get those things."

"No, I don't want you going to any trouble just for li'l old me."

We went into a shop that sold "authentic" antique Native weapons. I held up a tomahawk and said, "I wonder if they make these 'real' things as fast as those Hong Kong companies turn out fake Rolex watches."

Helene shook her head and tsked. "Clancy, you're just too cynical."

"Not cynical, just savvy. My mother used to put grated aspirin on my dessert and tell me it was sugar. I said, 'Mum, what kind of bullshit is that?'"

On our way back to the hotel, just as we exited the arcade, we got a surprise.

"Winnie Baxter! Inderjit Dhaliwal!" exclaimed Vicki as the two young women came into view. Vicki and her mum, seeing Inderjit's name in the list of players, had thought it merely a mistake, a printing error. But no; here she stood, still in the States, ready to play some more.

"Hey, Vicki," Winnie Baxter said. "Hey, Miz Vachon, Mister Wasserman."

Vicki smiled and nodded. Helene gave them a half-smile and looked away.

Winnie turned to me and said, "This is Inderjit Dhaliwal, my golfer friend from India."

Inderjit smiled and shook my hand. "I come from New Delhi. Have you seen my country?"

"Only on YouTube," I said. "Are you a terrorist?"

She gave a brisk shake of her head. "No, I am just a golfer. I am not wishing to crash planes into buildings. Indians not terrorists, just entrepreneurs."

"Inderjit," Winnie said, "has become infatuated with American culture. She wants to learn all she can."

Inderjit said, "Right on, bro! It's all good!"

Helene rolled her eyes. "Nice to see you. Gotta run."

"Did I tell you," Winnie said, "that I got a tattoo?"

"No," Vicki said. "Where is it?"

She slapped her backside. "Can't show you."

"Very nice," said Helene. "I'm sure your mum will be thrilled."

"She doesn't know about it. It's none of her business." To Vicki, Winnie said, "Break a leg tomorrow."

Vicki smiled. "You do the same."

As we walked away, we heard Inderjit call out, "USA, all the way! Red, white and blue rule! Yea!"

"I take it," Helene said to me, "that Inderjit is applying for a green card?"

21

Vicki drove, chopped and putted to a 68 with unfamiliar clubs, no caddy and little practice beforehand. She snarled and wiped sweat off her forehead under the brutal New Mexico sun. I drove the golf cart on the blacktop that snaked along the course.

"Stop this thing. I'm getting out." Helene climbed out of the cart and made a face at me. "And people bitch about *women* drivers."

"I'm not as bad as that," I retorted.

"You're even worse."

The golf cart, shiny and new, and mine for the day, had cost me no money. Newt Hoyle, director of the Go-4-It Open, had lent it to me. A flaccid, craggy faced septuagenarian, wore a tan-colored Stetson and a light-blue Western shirt, matching slacks and black boots. He had been in the Southwest all his life and served as the general manager of the resort and virtually everything surrounding it.

I liked Newt immensely and immediately. He hopped into the cart with me for Vicki's last nine holes and made no snide comments about my driving.

"Ya see, Clance," Newt explained, "I knew I could have all this here land for a resort as soon as I found a Native who could sign this and initial that on the paperwork. Then I took the paperwork to Uncle Sam, who gave me whatever the hell I wanted because Uncle Sam is afraid to say no to the Natives."

"Who was your first Native?" I asked.

"Can't Swim come first. He has enough sense to come in out of the rain. He brought in his friend Always Stoned, who can't tell the difference between midday and midnight. His momma sure named him right."

"Do you own all this?"

Newt shrugged. "Own some. Run most of it, but it mostly runs itself. Keeps me busy, and that's the main thing." Then, "Wow! You see that?"

Vicki had just hammered her tee shot onto the green, and her ball settled two dozen feet from the cup.

Newt pointed at Huey. "See that boy? He sure

looks like one of my employees. He's carrying her bag."

I nodded. "Yeah, her caddy failed to turn up, so your boy took the job."

"Some of them"—I knew he meant women—"sure can play golf, though they're not exactly built for it."

"She's Canadian, you know. Vicki Vachon from Ontario."

"That so? They must grow them cute up there."

"Yessiree," I said.

"Them girl golfers...do they like weenies or tacos?"

"Are you asking if they're lesbians?"

Newt arched an eyebrow. "That's *exactly* what I'm askin."

"Not so many lesbians now," I told him. "Not like before."

"That one." He nodded in Vicki's direction. "Boy, what a cutie. Pretty face. Real nice zoomers. Great ass. But she's as tall as a man. Be a damn shame if she ate pussy."

"Vicki is as straight as an arrow. Plus, she can beat

any man with a golf club."

Newt hooted. "Well, she can beat *my* club any day!"

We drove along for a few more holes and watched Vicki and Melinda Pardo, the woman with whom they had paired Vicki. Winnie Baxter and her partner, a Mexican American woman, were a couple of holes behind Vicki.

The scoreboard said that Vicki, in first place, led Winnie by two strokes. I hoped that Winnie wouldn't cave in and be abused by her crazy mum.

"Clancy," Newt was saying, "are you a betting man? I sure am."

"A man in your business? I thought you knew how hard it is to win in a casino."

"Casino betting don't interest me. They win, you lose. Where's the fun in that? I like to bet on golf. I'm an old man but I can play better than these younger shitasses."

"I don't doubt that," I said.

"My favorite people are the crack dealers. They come here, or they go to Vegas, with tote bags full of cash. They have no credit cards, just cash. Don't mean diddly to them if they lose their bets because they can easy get lots more cash."

"Do the crack dealers play golf well?"

"No, and they don't care. They're here for a good time, that's all. I have to show them the difference between a driver and a putter."

"Do you ever play the horses in Sussudio?"

"Can't play the horses. Animals are too unpredictable to bet on. I can figure out humans better than any shrink." Then, "Say, Clancy, are you married?"

"Hey?" I was watching Vicki sink a fifteen-foot putt. Going, going, gone. She pumped her fist; I smiled. That's my girl.

"I asked if you were married."

I shook my head. "Twice divorced."

"How come?"

I shrugged. "Long story."

"It's too bad when people get divorced. Been there, done that a few times myself. I'm as far from miserable now as I've ever been."

"'Far from miserable,' eh? I've never heard it put quite that way."

"Who did you marry, Clancy? A couple of white girls?"

I nodded. "How did you guess?"

"You shoulda married a gook."

"Why?"

"My wife's from Ho Chi Minh City, I think. Her name is Nguyen. You don't have to go all the way over there to get a gook wife, either. I found mine in southern California. They keep themselves clean, they work hard, they know how to treat a man. They don't yell and they don't tell and, oh, they're grateful as hell." He laughed. "Of course, most of them don't have much in the way of zoomers, but you can't have everything."

"I'll remember that, Newt."

"I see them gook women on TV now, too. Joan Chen, Lucy Liu. They're moving up in the world."

"They're Chinese, not Vietnamese," I told him.

"Chinese, Vietnamese, same thing, right?"

"Not exactly," I said.

"Maybe I should have held out for a Chinese woman," Newt said. "I notice they got bigger zoomers."

Newt and I sat in the golf cart behind the eighteenth green and enjoyed the clear view of Vicki as she stood at the tee. The scoreboard said that Winnie Baxter had finished with a 68, and I felt sure that she had some fans out there.

Very few people occupied the gallery, so I had an easy time spotting Helene as she traipsed in the general direction of Vicki. Helene's face looked shiny and she had sweated through her white golf shirt.

"There she is again," I muttered to Newt.

He nodded. "As fine a momma-and-girlie team as I've ever observed. Makes you want to go out and buy them fancy cars."

"New cars," I said, "make women hot and bothered."

"Have you screwed the baby momma yet?"

"I'm   not   sure   she   likes   me   that   way,

unfortunately," I said. "But she's pretty sexy, hey?"

Newt chuckled. "She'd make a dead man come."

"Helene and I are friends," I told him. "I like her daughter, too."

"In my experience, friendship with a woman means you'll never get to diddle her."

I laughed. "'Diddle.' I haven't heard that word in years."

"What do they say up there in Canada? 'Fuck' and 'screw'?"

Just then his cell phone rang.

"Newt here. Talk." He sighed. "Yeah, I heard ya. Yeah, yeah. Can't Swim and Always Stoned got something to do with this? Yeah, I figured. What a couple of assholes. I'll get on it." He sighed again as he put away his cell phone.

"Problem?" I asked.

"Yeah, I'd say there's trouble. Two local idiots, Raised by Snakes and Never Bathes, are trying to get Swim and Stoned to organize a protest out here. They want to have a thousand local Natives chanting and dancing and making a ruckus."

"What's their beef?"

"Well, they say that Candy Ass—that's Miles O'Connell, you know—when he come down here and design this golf course, he did so with the full knowledge of, and total indifference to, the fact that the eighteenth green is directly on sacred Native burial ground."

"Really?"

"Yep. Could be they're right, too."

"So, what are you going to do about it?" I asked.

He shrugged. "Wait and see what happens. Maybe they won't be dumb enough to piss me off even more. If they are, Lord help them."

22

Yolanda Rivera, the LPGA's current commissioner, had flown in and left messages for Helene and me to join her for dinner in one of the resort's many restaurants. Vicki had gone out to dinner downtown with Huey Clegg. "I want you to try some authentic Mexican food you probably can't find in Canada," he had said to her.

"The last time I checked out downtown Sussudio, their idea of authentic Mexican cuisine was Taco Bell," I told Helene.

We went together to have dinner with the commissioner, and Yolanda Rivers sat waiting for us in a dark jacket, black skirt and black T-shirt. She had short black hair and an olive complexion. She looked more handsome than pretty.

"Clancy Wasserman!" she exclaimed as she shook my hand. "I've read you in *CS* and am *thrilled* that you're now covering women's golf! I heard you were such a hit at Carver and Moe's Hottie jeans tournament. Don't you just *love* those two? Do you mind if I brag about us? Do you mind?"

"Well, *do* you?" Helene asked me.

"I *do* mind," I said, smirking.

Yolanda threw back her head and roared. "Funny guy! You Canadians crack me up! Are all you Canadians so funny?"

"Almost but not quite."

"Do you know why I'm so pleased you're here?" she asked rhetorically. "It's because this humble little event, the Go-4-It Classic, was *my* idea. Let's hear it for me!"

"Yea!" I said.

"Yea!" echoed Helene.

"And I'll tell you, in all sincerity, that I thought of this golf tournament while *drinking* a bottle of Go-4-It. That stuff, if I may say so, is like liquid crack—it just sets your neurons on fire. It's not the best-tasting beverage, of course, and the only reason I drank it was that we had been given a case of it, but it really gets you wired. So I thought, 'We need to have this company as a title sponsor.' So I called Morrie

Rosenthal, Go-4-It's marketing boss. You'll meet him soon enough. We've known each other for *years* and he's just a *super* guy. Now that we had the *what*, we needed the *where*. Out here in the Wild West seemed ideal. We chose Sussudio. I had heard of the Mescaline resort, but it still seemed anonymous and could do with some publicity. I called Newt Hoyle and ran it down for him. He said, 'Londie, let's do it!'"

This was one of those times when I wished I had gotten totally gooned before meeting someone.

The scowling teenage girl who took our drink orders wiped her nose, then wiped her hand on her crusty Levi's. She looked neither Native or Mexican; instead, she looked like a swarthy, sweaty, flunked-out-of-high-school kid who'd slept, doodled and daydreamed through her classes. I wanted a Manhattan over ice, but ordered a Coors because it would be easier for her to carry. Helene asked for a glass of Chardonnay.

"Newt's had to take a rain check," Yolanda said. "There's some issue with the golf course he needs to deal with right away."

"Trouble in paradise, eh?" I asked.

"Let's hope not." Yolanda had brought along a couple of her yes-women. "I'm sure you remember Clara from the Hottie tournament? And this is Breann Claudeson, my new deputy commissioner."

Breann, an unsmiling, slender woman, could have passed for attractive if she had lightened up a bit and put on some makeup. She said, "I'm glad to be Yolanda's second-in-command. This is a job where I know I can do some good. My golf background is perfect for the LPGA—I'm an expert on interpreting the rules. Also, I play a pretty mean game."

Just then, Morrie Rosenthal came in. Yolanda and Breann sprinted for him. They brought the Go-4-It honcho over me as soon as they got done fawning over him. Morrie, smooth and tanned, looked as if he'd had only one or two facelifts. He had on faded Levi's, loafers without socks and a T-shirt that read GOES DOWN GOOD. On the back, a likeness of a bottle of Go-4-It sort of explained the words on the front.

"Here he is!" Yolanda said as she presented Morrie to me. "Morrie, the man most responsible for making

Go-4-It the most popular energy drink in America. Clancy, how's Go-4-It doing in Canada?"

I shrugged. "Don't know. I've never actually looked for it up there."

"I have been bombarded with Go-4-It commercials all day," said Morrie, looking at Yolanda and snarling a bit at me. "We're utilizing all media and it's my job to sit through all those messages. Christ, I need a *drink*."

"Excuse us," I said, taking Helene by the arm and leading her away.

I felt surprised to see Kit Manley and Melinda Pardo there. "Why do you suppose they were invited?" I asked Helene.

"Because," she replied, keeping her voice down, "they are the two current player reps on the LPGA's board of directors."

"Nice for them."

"There are six other members of the board, but they're not here. Those others are big shots in business, but their names probably wouldn't mean much to you."

I nodded. "But they mean plenty to Yolanda. She

picked them herself and they'll side with her on every issue."

Helene smiled. "You're not as dumb as you look."

I smiled back. "Fuck you very much."

"In return for their tacit agreement to do as the commissioner wishes, the board members get stuff," she told me.

"What kinda stuff?"

"Perks."

"What kinda perks?"

"Free trips to major golf resorts throughout North America. Trips to Europe, four-star hotels. The kinds of things only travel agents used to get."

"And popular Canadian sportswriters," I said.

"Really? Have you gotten those kinds of trips?"

"Yeah, and I didn't have to sit through boring meetings or kiss anyone's ass."

"Right," she said. "You just flew out to meet up with some superstar athlete. You hung out together and then you wrote about the experience."

I smirked. "Nice work if you can get it, eh?" Then, "Let's go say hello to Kit and Melinda."

Helene nodded. "Lead the way."

...

I had never introduced myself to, nor shaken hands with, Kit Manley or Melinda Pardo; still, they acted as if we were old acquaintances and asked me how I'd liked the Hottie Classic.

"You're doing a story on Vicki Vachon, too, right?" asked Kit Manley.

"That's why I followed her and her mum from the Hottie," I replied.

Melinda Pardo had gotten all dressed up in a dress and fancy shoes. Her hair tumbled about her shoulders and her push-up bra reminded me of what a fine pair of zoomers she owned. Kit Manley had put on a T-shirt, blazer and khaki slacks. She'd gone to the barber shop and come out looking like one of the Beatles.

"Vicki is awesome," said Kit Manley. "She is just what ladies' golf has been waiting for. Talented, charismatic and gorgeous."

Melinda Pardo nodded. "She is a huge credit to our sport."

"Hey!" Kit Manley exclaimed. "Here's someone else you need to meet! Laurent, come over! Laurent Reboul, our special guest, these people are Clancy Wasserman and Helene Vachon. He's the sportswriter from Canada and she's the mother of Vicki Vachon, the golfer."

Laurent Reboul offered us tiny nods but no handshake.

Kit Manley said, "Laurent is from France."

"Paris," said Laurent.

"Which part of Paris?" asked Kit.

"The best parts," answered Laurent.

"Laurent," continued Kit, "was recently named one of the world's richest people by *Money* magazine."

"It's true," said Laurent.

"Nice for you," I said.

Helene smiled.

"Laurent went to some trouble," explained Kit, "to be with us today. We flew on his Learjet from his home in Paris."

"I have more than one Learjet," interjected Laurent, "just as I have more than one home."

"Will you give me a ride back to Canada?" I asked.

"Laurent flew all the way out here for the big news that Yolanda is going to spring on us tonight," said Kit. "Then she'll go into some detail at the press conference tomorrow."

"Big news, eh?" I asked. "I *love* big news. Spill it!"

Kit laughed. "You'll love it, Clancy. But you'll have to wait like everyone else.."

"Promise it will be *big news?*"

"Oh, yeah." Kit nodded. "You'll *love* it, dude."

23

I'm still angry about how, on my twelfth birthday, my parents served us roast beef and Yorkshire pudding, my brother's favorite dinner but not mine. I have always dreaded being served an evening meal I disliked, and at many dinner parties and industry luncheons, the menu items I have had to choose from included liver and onions, tripe, perogies and other things that make me gag.

So, when Yolanda Rivera got us all seated in her private room and told us she had ordered for all of us. I guessed that I would dislike whatever she was about to have them serve me. I was right.

Veggie lasagna.

But I had learned from the past. Before going to this dinner, I had eaten a huge chicken-and-cheese burrito, pushed aside my plate of veggie lasagna and declined on the slimy, yogurty dessert.

Yolanda stood and tapped her glass with her spoon. "Attention, please, everyone. What I am about to tell you is the biggest news I have had in a long time. It will also be the biggest news you've heard in quite a while. It is *huge*."

"Absolutely," said Breann Claudeson, sitting to her boss's right.

"Tomorrow morning will not just be any springtime Friday," Yolanda said. "The global media will awaken the world with the news that Reboul Enterprises of Paris is the new owner of Kraft Foods. Yes! That's right! Kraft, the world's largest manufacturer of food products, is now a part of the Reboul empire!"

The rest of the audience and I gave Reboul some tentative, halfhearted applause, as if unsure that his acquisition of Kraft was altogether a good thing.

Laurent Reboul acknowledged our applause with a tentative, halfhearted nod.

"Naturally," Yolanda went on, "the financial specifics of the deal are known only to Laurent and the sellers, but tomorrow I will talk about these things in more detail. You'll be glad to know that Clara has arranged to have some very powerful media representatives present for tomorrow morning. In fact, at this moment we have our good friend Clancy Wasserman from *Canadian Sports* magazine. Our very own Breann Claudeson will make sure that *USA Today* knows what's going on."

"Absolutely," said Breann.

Morrie Rosenthal, who'd already downed a few cocktails, said, "Sometimes I wish I had a hardscrabble childhood I needed to overcome. But I didn't. I was spoiled rotten from birth."

"Could we please get on with it?" Laurent Reboul asked.

"Of course." Yolanda cleared her throat and got serious. "Laurent, as you probably know, owns a company that is the world's largest maker of pet food. He is very proud of his success in that industry, as well he should be, because he has kept the world's cats and dogs healthy and happy for years. That has been the source of much of his wealth.

"Now that he owns Kraft Foods, Laurent, by default, has acquired the Kraft Nabisco Golf Tournament. He will increase the purse by one million dollars. Furthermore, we have unanimously approved Laurent's proposal to rename the event the Reboul Classic. That is how next week's tournament, the first major one of the season, will be known from here on out. A sudden change, yes, but these things were done in the boardroom and the media ideally won't misspell 'Reboul' too often.

"Also, the trophy will have a new name: the Reboul Cup. For so many years, it was named for Dinah Shore, but she left us two decades ago and Laurent feels we should live in the present and put the past to rest. Indeed, Laurent has said he believes that relatively few people of significance in golf know, or care, about who Dinah Shore was.

"Naturally, we will be sad to see the Open leave Mission Hills, its home since the early Seventies, but Laurent has bought the Hollywood Sun Country Club in Palm Springs, an aging course lovingly restored to youthfulness by the acclaimed architect Miles O'Connell.

"Am I perturbed," Yolanda asked us rhetorically, "by the fact that our tour has a new sponsor who has made his fortune from pet food? Hardly. As you may know, the main ingredient in pet food is horse meat, and one of Laurent's ambitions is to make that product a staple in American households. Europeans have been enjoying it for years, and if it's good enough for them, maybe we should give it a try."

Yolanda looked around the room for a moment and said, "Well, there it is."

24

I hate computers and they hate me. For someone in my job, computers are necessary, and that sucks.

I say this because, after breakfast, I had nothing to do except wait for Vicki Vachon and Winnie Baxter, whose tee time was one-thirty, so I went back to my room to boot up my laptop, go online, check my emails and find out if maybe Britney Spears was having another baby.

But when I turned on my laptop, as I had done hundreds of times before, it did something new and wanted: its screen turned midnight blue and endless lines of code appeared. No matter what I did, I couldn't get the screen to change color or the code to fuck off.

I French-kissed it and masturbated it and said it was the most beautiful computer ever made. I said, "Wake up, baby. Daddy needs you." I hit every combination of keys, then slapped it upside the head and yelled, "You bitch! Wake up and get your shit together before I throw you out the window!"

Finally I picked up the house telephone and dialed Vicki and Helene's number.

"Do you ladies know anything about computers?" I asked Helene. "Mine is copping a major attitude right now."

"I don't know bits from bytes," Helene told me, "but Vicki does all our computer stuff, and whenever we have a snafu, she fixes it herself."

"I don't like to make *my* problem *yours*, but some weird virus has gotten into my machine and I have this little thing called a *livelihood* that's sort of at stake."

"She's getting dressed right now, but I'll send her over to your room."

"I really don't like to bug you on a game day—"

"No problem. Just don't keep her too long. She needs to putt and drive balls for an hour so she can get 'mentally together.'"

"I hear ya. If she says that my computer is permanently catatonic, I'll trash the machine and see if there's a nearby Apple dealer."

Five minutes later, I heard a knock at the door.

"Computer virus lady is here," Vicki said, carrying her own laptop. She looked gorgeous in an argyle sweater and gray slacks.

"Thanks so much for your help," I told her. "Maybe this is going to turn out to be something minor or it will be something major. I certainly hope it's minor. All I know about computers is how to turn them on and off and send a file. I can do as little of that stuff as my job requires."

Vicki grinned. "You're about as computer-friendly as most people your age."

She put her machine alongside mine and played around with jacks and cords, plugging in here, unplugging there. Then she sat down, opened up my laptop and guffawed.

"What's funny?" I asked.

"That blue screen. Really freaks you out, eh?"

"Tell me about it. You've seen this screen before?"

"Lots and lots of times," she said. Her fingers flew across my keyboard and her own. I thought of Diana Krall, playing the piano during a concert in Bayporte.

"Can you fix it?" I asked.

"That's what I'm doing."

"That's totally excellent," I said. "That's insanely magnificent. Will you tell the little bitch never to do anything like this again?"

"If you like." She did her Diana Krall thing some more. "There it is. Mission accomplished."

I bent over and looked at my screen. It had backed off with its attitude and was ready for honest work again.

"Wow!"

"You know, Clancy," Vicki said, "I don't have to go just yet. How about buying me a pop?"

"I'll buy you whatever you desire."

"A pop would be nice."

I went into my minibar, took out a Coke and handed it to her. She opened it and took a long swallow.

Vicki said, "I want to tell you something, Clancy. My mum really likes you a lot."

"Your mum is a lovely lady. I like her, too."

"But," Vicki wanted to know, "do *you* like *her* the same way *she* likes *you*?"

"How do you know she likes me that way?"

She shrugged. "Oh, little things. She's smoking like a bloody chimney and she won't talk about you."

I laughed.

"I'm not kidding," she said. "She smokes to cope with things like men who turn her on. I say, 'How's Clancy?' and she says, 'Same as before.' I say, 'He's a rad guy,' and she says, 'I guess.' I say, 'I'm surprised he's divorced; he's good-looking,' and she says, 'Oh, do you think he's good-looking?' I say, 'What do you talk about with him?' and she says, 'This and that.' I ask, 'If you're not interested in him, why do you take so long to get yourself together before you see him?' and she says, 'I don't know what you're talking about.'"

"Has she done much dating since her divorce?"

"Some. She says she's met some real goofs and idiots that way."

"Too bad. What about your dad?"

She narrowed her eyes a bit. "What about him?"

"Tell me about him."

"Why?"

"Because I really wanna know."

"Is your interest professional or personal?" she asked.

I smiled. "Both. But mostly I'm asking because I'm the guy your mum likes so much."

"My dad"—she spat out the words—"is human scum."

I looked at her and she glowered at me.

"He's a liar, a thief and a bully," she added.

"Is that what *you* think of him or are you just repeating what your mum has said?"

"Neither of us has any use for him."

I nodded. "Your mum said he took money that was rightfully yours."

"He was born bad and will die that way. I hate to speak of him that way, because he's my own father, but I hate to *think* of him that way too—that he is my own father and I have his genes. I guess I think of him the way Charles Manson's children think of their father."

"Charles Manson?" I guffawed. "I don't think your father is as bad as all that."

Vicki glowered again at me. "Well, you're not my father's daughter." Then, "My mum is gorgeous, charming, smart, a hard worker. Makes me wonder how he got her, then let her get away."

"For all your father's flaws," I told her, "I don't think he was poor, dumb and ugly."

She laughed despite herself. "I guess you have a point."

"Also, your mum is so lucky to have you in her life. You're mother and daughter, but you're also the best of friends. Do you know how many young daughters have told their mums to fuck off?"

"The girls who say that to their mums don't have one like mine. She's *so* easy to get along with. My father had no respect for her dignity. She abused her. I don't know if he punched her out, but he definitely browbeat her and treated her like a second-class citizen. She deserved much better than the life she had with him."

"But he turned you on to golf, right?"

She shook her head. "*Mum* did."

"But the media stories said—"

"'Daddy taught me' reads better than 'Mummy taught me.' She saw me fiddling with the clubs when I was seven or eight, and she saw right away that I had a good natural motion. So we'd go out to the public courses and play all day. She had watched so many tournaments and read so many golf magazines that she had a hundred tips for me. She wanted me to get really interested in something like golf I wouldn't smoke crack or let boys feel me up all night." She sighed and smiled. "We had *so* much fun, Clancy. You can't imagine."

"How did your father like it when his little girl became a competitive golfer?"

"Oh, he *hated* it. All that attention *I* got meant people paid less attention to *him*. He was a fairly competent golfer, too, but never potential PGA material. The funny thing was, once I started winning amateur competitions, he took full credit for my success."

"Is he in your life at all now?"

She shrugged. "He calls sometimes. He'll say, 'Congrats on winning that tournament,' and then go on about the mistakes I made." She paused. "I guess I really don't hate him and I don't think he's all that bad. I think, deep down inside, that he can't help himself. He's just a goof."

I checked my watch and said, "You still have time to hit a few practice balls. But I want to ask you a few more questions."

"About Winnie?"

"Well, yes."

"I don't know why she would want to harm me. She's the closest thing to a friend I have on the tour. The only thing that freaks me is, my mum half-believes that Winnie might be out to get me."

"And you always trust your mum's judgment, right?"

Vicki nodded.

"What about that Indian girl?"

"Inderjit? I don't know anything about her. She's from, where? India? Pakistan? I don't know where those places are. She's the worst golfer I've ever met." She smirked. "If she's the best India has, maybe they should stick to making movies and taking over the world economy."

"Do you like Winnie's mum?"

Vicki thought for a moment. "Dawn? She's always been nice to me, but I wouldn't turn my back on her for too long."

"You better get out there and hit a few balls," I said.

"Guess so."

"Go out there and win this one for the Great White North."

We exchanged a high five and she gave me her biggest, winningest smile. "Fuckin' A!"

25

Winnie Baxter played well and shot the lowest score she had in a long time at the Go-4-It Open. But I knew she would have an issue with her mother as soon as Dawn saw that tattoo on her daughter's bum. Winnie looked focused and determined as she drove and putted her way through the afternoon, but even her Kurt Cobain sunglasses couldn't completely hide the swelling and discoloration around her right eye or the puffiness around her jawline. Her movements at times seemed a bit tentative, as if Mum Baxter, after slapping the girl's face a few dozen times, decided to kick her limbs, too. Winnie, while lacking Vicki's height and strength, was a decent size herself; certainly she could have warded off her mother's face and body blows.

Helene and I sat in the cart. "I'll ride with you," she'd said, "if you'll let me do the driving." Dawn Baxter spent the day in the Vicki/Winnie gallery. We caught up with her and Helene asked about Winnie.

Dawn tsked. "I tell you, that girl has been accident prone since birth. She got out of the shower, slipped on the floor and landed on her face."

"How awful for her," said Helene.

I shook my head in empathy. "Hard luck, eh?"

Presently we drove off.

"Dawn Baxter is a lying bitch," said Helene.

"I wonder how her husband feels about her."

"He's married to his job," she said. "He keeps forgetting he has a wife, too."

"Vicki should aim one of her tee shots at Dawn and brain the bitch," I said.

"Hey, that's not a bad idea," Helene retorted, laughing. "I'll take it up with her."

Winnie is no loser, I thought as I watched her play despite her swollen face and injured limbs. Through the first nine holes she stayed focused, made par and pumped her fist each time her putt went in. Only Vicki played better golf that day.

Kit Manley and Melinda Pardo trailed Vicki and

Winnie, and a few Mexican Americans were a couple of shots behind Kit and Melinda. Nobody else presented a threat to Vicki. All of them sneered at the cold gusts of wind that made Mescaline such a challenging course. The top players, men and women, had something bad to say about this course.

At the end of the course we spotted Inderjit Dhaliwal in the Vicki/Winnie gallery. The Indian girl had finished over 70, an abysmal score, and decided she'd had enough.

Inderjit saw us. She smiled, waved and came over.

"Why did you withdraw?" Helene asked her.

"I am not playing good golf," Inderjit replied. "My score is being much too high. I am being a follower of friends now. I am cheering them on." She pumped her arm and exclaimed, "Go, Vicki!"

"That's the first intelligent thing I've heard you say," Helene muttered.

Inderjit frowned and looked at me. Helene pressed on the accelerator and off we went.

Vicki finished under 70, the only golfer to do so on Friday, and her score put her ahead of Winnie Baxter by several strokes in the tournament. Going into Saturday's final eighteen holes, Winnie had toughed it out in those adverse conditions and had a score of 72.

Helene and I sat in the cart and watched Vicki and Winnie play their eighteenth. Vicki rolled in a two-footer as if she'd been doing so all her life, then plucked the ball out of the cup and stepped aside.

Another cart pulled up alongside us.

"How-dee!" called out Newt Hoyle. He tugged at his dark Stetson and pointed at his dark Western suit. "Like my duds?"

"Not especially," I replied, "but it doesn't matter what I think."

He stuck a thumb at the lady sitting next to him. "This is Billie. Billie, these folks are Clancy and Helene. They're from Canada. Do you know where that is?"

"Fuck you, Newt, I ain't that dumb," retorted Billie.

"Billie helps me run my empire," Newt explained. "She's been with me longer than any woman I've been married to."

"Damn straight," said Billie. "And I've been more

of a wife to him than any of those bimbos he wedded."

"I was her savior," Newt told us. "I rescued her while she was playing piano in a Detroit bar. She was the only white girl there and all the spooks were checking her out. Not sure why I was there. I was probably up to no good, myself. Anyway, I was glad to get her out of there with me."

"You didn't 'save' me from nothin," Billie said. "I was singin Stevie Wonder songs and the crack dealers were stickin twenties into my jar."

Billie, a svelte lady in pleated slacks and a pullover sweater, had hair that had been teased and sprayed till it stood up an entire foot, as if her hairdresser were still living in the Sixties. A feared a bird might fly by and make its home in there.

Newt said, "I heard Reboul the Frenchie and Yolanda the lady boss left town already. They took off for Pebble Beach or someplace in his jet. I wish they'd stayed around longer. I like being near rich people, so that if they drop something, I can pick it up."

"They're careful not to drop anything," said Billie.

"That's why they're rich."

"It's a good thing," Newt said, "that my big brother Benji isn't here. He's hated them Frenchies since World War Two, and he still talks about them. I was too young for that, but he believed in defending Old Glory so he went over there and got shot up a bit. I like to brag about his sometimes."

"Well, at least he made it back home alive," I said.

Newt laughed. "Hell, it would take more than a few Nazi bullets to bring old Benji down. Once he got back home, all he wanted to talk about was the Frenchies and how they couldn't fight for shit. He would go to the movies and couldn't understand how Hollywood was making them out to be heroes and such. Benji said all the Frenchies was good for was cooking and making love."

He added that his missus was due back soon. He invited us to dinner with them. "They serve you a good barbecue meal in the Apache Room. Be sure to bring Wonder Girl with you."

"Wonder Girl," said Helene, "usually has dinner in her room with me, her mother."

"And I have a bunch of computer work to do," I

told him.

"Then I'll see ya when I see ya," Newt said. "Give my best to Wonder Girl."

"Apache Room," I said as Helene and I cruised away. "Barbecue. Sounds yummy."

"Newt ought to go back to Texas," Helene remarked.

"He called Vicki 'Wonder Girl.' Maybe *we* should start calling her that."

"Fuck that," Helene said.

I got a message to call Kerry Gaines, my boss in Toronto.

Although it would be getting late back east, I knew he'd still be in his office at *CS*. Every other Friday, he liked to stay late, ostensibly to demonstrate to everyone his willingness to be the last one out. Actually, he liked sitting up there alone, twenty stories above Toronto, so he could visit Internet porn sites instead of driving home to spend time with his grumpy wife and spoiled children.

Once he grew tired of the porn sites, he would walk over to the Windsor Hotel, where the company kept a room, and take a Ryerson University journalism coed to dinner. Ideally she would be a passably pretty white girl who had already figured out that the best way to advance professionally was to put out for powerful people like Kerry Gaines.

"Clancy! How's it in sunny California?" he asked.

"Beats me. I'm in New Mexico."

"New Mexico, eh? They got some pretty little women there and I'm gonna get me one," he sang.

"Kerry, why are you calling?"

"One of my sources told me about Reboul, the guy who just bought Kraft. We should say something about it. Think you can handle it?"

By "sources," Kerry meant editors. A hack is a writer. Of course, some editors also write—the former started out as the latter—and the editors who are unaware that they have forgotten how to write will often pull up the hack's copy and goof it up with clichés before publishing it.

Researchers have an important-sounding title, but they mostly just call around to check facts.

Photographers, of course, take pictures. Account executives, the people who sell ads, know that they're far more valuable than hacks like me who write "stuff" about the sports stars of the moment.

"Yeah, I'll do it," I told Kerry. "I've met Reboul."

"Really? What did you think of him?"

"He's another guy who thinks his shit doesn't stink."

"Well, our readers don't have to know about *that*. Say, how's that piece going about the sexy Canadian golfer?"

"She's about to win her second consecutive competition."

"Her name's Trixie, right?"

"Vicki," I said.

"Trixie sounds better."

"I wouldn't call her that to her face."

<u>26</u>

The chanting I heard at the eighteenth hole sounded so much like Eminem or Ice-T's blather that I wanted to whip out my iPhone, record them and get the footage on YouTube, just to see how many views I would get.

Naturally, not everyone there was a Native, but I spotted Can't Swim and Always Stoned right away. Both men looked as if they'd gone to the Sally Ann clothing store and bought whatever would clash the most. Can't Swim wore a maroon velvet suit, green Nikes, an orange dress shirt, broad yellow tie and a Castrol Oil snapback cap. Always Stoned had on a black satin bomber jacket advertising a rock music station in the Midwest. He also wore khaki cargo shorts, high-top runners and a gray fedora.

"Those two look ridiculous," Helene said as we sat in the cart.

"Tell that to them," I replied.

We listened for a bit to the chanting, which sounded like, "Ooga chaka, ooga chaka."

"What do you suppose it means?" Helene asked.

"I don't know their language, but I guess they're saying, 'Lord, please send these white people back to Europe so we can have our home again.'"

Helene laughed. Then, "I'm getting worried about Vicki again. She's getting too bloody smug, thinking she's already won the tournament and can just take it easy out there. Winnie will probably throw a temper tantrum or burst into tears if things don't go her way."

"Vicki doesn't have a huge lead," I said, "and the lead she *does* have could disappear very fast if she hits a bad tee shot or misses a couple of putts. I've seen that happen a hundred times. If Vicki blows her lead and doesn't win this thing, it will be nobody's fault but her own."

"Fuck you, Clancy," Helene said, and we both chuckled.

The weather that day was ideal for golf—sunny, cloudless, windless. Vicki wore a white golf shirt, matching shorts and white golf shoes. Winnie wore a yellow top, black shorts and yellow shoes.

On the first nine holes, the flags looked so far away that I thought they might be in Arizona. Vicki appeared small and girlish as she teed up her shots. She whacked her balls into those vast valleys and ended up with a couple of bogeys. Winnie made par for each of Vicki's bogeys.

"Vicki's lead is almost nothing now," Helene said. "This is just the kind of thing that always freaks me out." She lit a Player's Light.

"But she's playing good golf. You should be proud of her," I said.

"I'll be proud of her when they give her that goddamn trophy and we can get out of his godforsaken place," she muttered.

I chortled.

"That guy who's her caddy?" Helene said between drags from her cigarette. "Huey Clegg? He's not doing her much good out there."

I shrugged. "He's doing his best for her. He can

only carry her clubs, not swing them for her."

"Well, duh."

We stayed as far out of Vicki's sight as possible but noticed Dawn Baxter in the gallery, just s few feet from Winnie, the mother's arms crossed and mouth set in an "I dare you to fuck up" look.

Vicki and Winnie's followers, a few hundred at least, stood in clusters here and there and past the greens.

"Where's Inderjit?" Helene asked me. "I don't see her anywhere."

"She's probably on the practice range, learning to golf," I replied. Then I pointed and added, "There's Breann Claudeson, the deputy commissioner."

"I'm sure she's sort of decided she's the boss around here, in her blue blazer and khaki slacks, with all those radios and cell phones she's carrying."

"I wonder if she has a gun," I said.

"She doesn't need one. She could kick all our asses with one foot."

Just then, another cart pulled up alongside us.

"Hey, guys!" called out Morrie Rosenthal, Go-4-It's marketing boss. "Are we having fun yet?"

"As long as my kid stays in the lead," Helene said, "I'm having a perfectly lovely time."

Morrie, the professional diplomat, laughed. "As long as Vicki keeps her cool and plays it one stroke at a time, she'll be OK. But Winnie's not giving up, huh? Usually she does, but not this time. Makes for good drama."

"I still think Winnie will choke and lose this event," I said. "I think her mother believes it too. They both find this choking thing to be totally humiliating."

"It's not too much fun for the fans to watch, either," Morrie observed.

Then we watched as Vicki handed Huey her club and hurried off the fairway. She disappeared into the trees, and we figured she had been caught short. The courses always have portable toilets nearby for this very reason.

When Vicki remained AWOL after several minutes, we drove onto the fairway and stopped a foot from the deputy commissioner.

"Is there a time limit for potty breaks?" I asked her.

"Excuse me?" Breann Claudeson frowned.

"Vicki," Helene said, "has been off the course for close to ten minutes. Aren't you alarmed?"

"If she takes much longer," Breann replied, "I'll penalize her for delay of play."

Helene shook her head in frustration and we sped off towards the toilets. We got out of the car and hiked up an incline. The toilets soon came into view and so did Vicki, who stood rubbing her backside and muttering.

"What happened?" Helene asked. "Are you all right?"

"Somebody hit me with something," Vicki said.

"Hit you? How?" Helene wanted to know.

"I didn't see them. I think they were trying to hit me below the bum, to hurt my sciatic nerve, but they missed."

"So you have *no* idea who attacked you," said Helene, with a disappointed sigh.

"Definitely someone who wanted her to lose this

golf match," I put in.

"That Indian girl. Inderjit," said Helene.

"You mean that?" I asked.

"No, I'm just bullshitting. Of *course* I'm serious."

"But you can't prove it," I pointed out.

Vicki rubbed her bottom some more. "It's starting to hurt less now. Like I said, good thing they got me in the ass instead of the leg."

"Maybe," said Helene, "we should take you to a doctor."

Vicki shook her head. "No doctors. It's not that big a deal. Let's just play golf."

Breann Claudeson joined us. She said, "Now, what's our problem?"

"I fell on my ass," Vicki said.

"Well, not exactly," Helene interjected. "But I'll tell you all about it later. In fact, I'll tell Yolanda about it, too."

"You'll tell us *what*?" Breann asked.

"I'll tell you both," said Helene, "when Yolanda arrives."

Breann shrugged and turned to Vicki. "Are you ready to continue playing?"

"Yes," said Vicki.

"No," said Helene.

"Mum," Vicki said through gritted teeth, "I'm fucking *playing*. Understand?"

27

I'm wondering where I would rank Vicki's performance in the last several holes of the Go-4-It energy drink tournament. Certainly it was among the finest I'd ever seen, and I had seen plenty of spectacular rounds of play. I watched with admiration as Vicki, despite her sore bum and temporarily—I hoped—traumatized psyche from the attack.

Her first sore-bum shot was from the tee on the fifteenth green. I could tell from the way she half-wriggled her fanny that it was still on the disabled list, and she didn't hit the ball as hard as necessary. Her ball ended up a dozen meters short of the green.

Fortunately for Vicki, Winnie's tee shot went directly into the rough and she faced a long, difficult second shot to get into decent putting range.

When Vicki made a terrific shot that got to within ten feet of the cup, Helene cheered, pumped her arm and looked at the cart's steering wheel for a horn to honk.

But Helene quit celebrating when Winnie's next shot, hit much too hard and apparently headed off the course entirely, instead slammed into the flagstick, did a weird little bobbling dance and fell into the cup.

"What a fluke!" Helene screamed. "I don't believe it! Somebody up there hates me!"

I looked over to the crowd on the other side of the fairway. Dawn Baxter stood there, doing her own little victory dance, arms pumping, hips rocking.

"Winnie," said Helene, "is going to pull it out. no choking this time. It was just meant to be. There's nothing we can do about it. Shit."

"It ain't over till it's over," I told her.

"What?"

"It ain't over till the fat lady sings," I said.

"What *are* you babbling about?"

"Vicki is still ahead, Helene. The contest isn't over. Wait till it's a done deal before you get all emotional one way or the other."

She just shrugged. Then she started up the cart again and drove us to the sixteenth hole, which featured a canyon that looked half a mile deep. Miles

O'Connell—Candy Ass to the locals—liked to build canyons and waterfalls on golf courses, and he liked to steal other architects' ideas for golf courses. Many people laughed at the courses he designed, but many more hired him to build their courses.

Winnie prepared to tee off first.

"Winnie looks totally together," Helene observed. "By now she's usually shaking or crying or something."

"Is the girl's presence of mind a bad thing?" I asked her.

"Whose side are you on?" she asked, glowering. But her question had some validity. I felt full of anxiety, panic and dread, and I was just supposed to be a disinterested journalist covering a golf match.

Winnie hit her tee ball, and while it didn't look so great—her tee shots were never much to brag about—her ball went where it needed to go, and it settled thirty or forty feet from the flag.

"Decent shot. Too bad," murmured Helene.

"Vicki's up next."

"This hole sucks. This course sucks. New Mexico sucks. I can't watch."

"Then close your eyes," I said.

She did.

The mum kept her face buried in her hands as the daughter smashed her ball into the sky and called out, "Yeah! Go baby!"

Her ball sought out the center of the green, found it and stayed put.

"That damn brat of yours," I said to Helene, "is going to give me a heart attack."

Both golfers two-putted the hole and made par, but then Helene found something else to *kvetch* about.

"This hole coming up? It's worse than the one we just finished. The way this one is shaped, if she hits it and it goes left, the ball is going to bounce down Main Street in Sussudio."

"Then she better make damn sure she hits it straight," I said.

Helene crossed her fingers as Winnie stepped up and yanked her ball way off to the left. "Yea!" the golf mum yelled. "The ball is going shopping! Vicki will win!"

But then she watched in dismay as the wayward ball struck the tall bunker and stayed on the course.

Helene blew out a huge sigh. "Shit! She's not in bad shape at all. She's damn lucky that bunker is so tall."

"Helene," I said, "the bunker is to tall for that very reason—to catch the bad shots shitty golfers make."

She snarled at me a bit and said, "I knew that."

Vicki hauled off and hit another moonshot. This one went a bit farther to the left than she would have probably liked, but the ball corrected itself and landed thirty feet from the cup. Even with a sore bum, she could hit a golf ball nearly 300 meters.

"Try to beat *that*, Winnie Baxter," Helene muttered.

Winnie, still in the bunker, made a frustrated swipe at her ball and very nearly knocked it into downtown, but her ball instead hit a lone, scarred tree and caromed off onto the green. It kept moving until it petered out about thirty feet from the cup.

"What the *fuck*," Helene said under her breath. "Too ludicrous. Totally outrageous."

When Vicki's next shot got her to within five feet of the cup, I whispered, "She's still probably going to gain a stroke on Winnie when she sinks this five-footer."

Helene nodded and crossed her fingers.

Alas, golf can be a cruel, heartless, maddening game that sometimes allows luck to triumph over talent.

Winnie's hands shook with anxiety as she addressed her thirty-footer. Her posture was bad, her swing uneven and hit her ball too hard. Nevertheless, her ball, as if it had eyes of its own and knew where to go, drunkenly wandered in the right direction for thirty feet and, after pausing for a moment or two on the lip of the cup, dropped in. Then Vicki's no-brainer putt refused to do likewise.

Vicki lined up her putt and hit it just so. Her ball headed for the cup, then inexplicably floated right over it. Vicki cocked her hip insolently, kicked at the air and glanced over at Huey, who offered her a tiny shrug. Then she traipsed over to her ball and tapped it in, ignoring the trickle of applause from her gallery.

Weird birdie for Winnie. Hard luck for Vicki.

The two were now tied as they went to the final hole.

I looked over and spotted Dawn Baxter doing her

little dance again.

In our cart, Helene slammed the palm of her hand into the steering wheel before stomping on the accelerator and taking us to where Winnie and Vicki's tee shots would land.

"I can see that you're angry," I said, turning to Helene. "Anger and greed are very underrated emotions. I like to hate politicians, sports stars and editors because it lets me put my rage on specific targets. I cope better that way."

Helene frowned in bemusement. "I'm not feeling anger or hate. I'm feeling pity."

I arched my eyebrows. "Pity?"

She nodded. "Pity. Do you want to hear about it?"

I nodded. "Do tell."

"I'm feeling pity for Dawn and Winnie because *they* have to be *them* while *I* get to be *me*."

"Ouch!"

She looked past me and said, "Check that out. Par-four eighteenth hole. No bunkers, no water, no obstacles. No challenge. You can tee off and it doesn't matter where you hit it, you'll be OK. What was Miles O'Connell thinking when he designed it like that?"

"He was thinking, 'I'll make this last hole nice and easy so that even the worst golfer can finish playing with a smile on his face.'"

We both watched Winnie Baxter as she stood at the tee, took a vicious hack and very nearly missed the ball altogether. She reminded me of all the baseball hitters I had seen foul off pitches.

"Oh *wow*," Helene murmured, her hand cupped over her mouth, as we watched Winnie's ball bounce and roll about a hundred yards along the ground.

Helene said nothing more. I said nothing, and neither did anyone else. Winnie stood there, as if quite unable to believe what she'd just done.

Vicki, who probably wanted to jump for joy at the sight of her rival's botched tee shot, simply went up her own ball and drove it nearly 300 meters, exchanged a high five with Huey Clegg and the two of them marched down the fairway.

I felt so sad for Winnie as I watched her slash again at her ball and make it travel another 50 meters or so. Then, for her third shot, she hit it again and we watched it go a bit farther. She paused and stared at the little white ball that had suddenly become her worst enemy, and everyone grew silent or just murmured to each other.

Vicki, perhaps out of pity for Winnie, seemed in a bit of a hurry to make her par three, and she did just that, sinking her par putt, plucking it out of the cup and tipping her cap to the crowd. The only thing left for us to do was to watch Winnie's implosion continue. She kept hitting her ball poorly, not out of rage or frustration, but out of simple incompetence, as if she'd suddenly forgotten everything she had ever learned about golf. By and by she made it within putting range and, three tries later, finally tapped her ball into the cup.

"So sad," Helene said as we sat in the cart. "So tragic to see her fall apart in front of everyone." Then she burst into a giggling fit. Upon recovering, she said, "Would you hate me if I told you I enjoyed every moment of watching Winnie fuck up?"

"I could *never* hate you, Helene."

She giggled some more as we got out of the cart. Then she threw her arms around me and kissed my lips. She gave me a long, friendly kiss, the kind that said, 'Don't worry. I've got plenty more of *these* for you.'

That kiss meant a great deal to me, but Helene had bigger things to get excited about. The golf world had something to talk about: two consecutive wins for Vicki Vachon on the LPGA Tour. Sexy Canadian teenager with hurt bum still wins the damn thing, and does so just a week before the first major in southern California. Vicki Vachon was hot, hot, hot.

When Vicki dropped in her final putt for the Go-4-It Open victory, she looked in her mum's direction and raised her fist like a Caucasian female Black Panther.

Helene did likewise and called out, "You go, girl!"

Vicki then rubbed a bit at her sore rump as she walked over to shake Winnie's hand. But Winnie ran in the other direction, afraid of the beating her mother would inflict upon her very soon.

28

Not too long ago, Newt Hoyle and Morrie Rosenthal had argued over how the Go-4-It trophy should look. Newt told me that he wanted the trophy to be a hatchet of some kind mounted on a plaque, because that would say, 'Native American.' Morrie wanted the plaque to have a replica of his company's energy drink. Morrie backed off after Newt said their discussions were wearing him out and, with one telephone call, he could have one of his boys track Morrie down and shove a can of Go-4-It up the marketing wizard's ass.

Vicki's prize, an ancient tomahawk mounted on a polished mahogany plaque, looked handsome and dignified, even if the tomahawk was hardly ancient and scarcely looked like a war weapon.

Golf fans and Natives watched with much interest as Vicki received her due. Helene and I sat on folding chairs inside the ropes, next to Newt Hoyle, Billie Who Helps Newt, Can't Swim and Always Stoned. If

Winnie Baxter had played a half-decent eighteenth hole, they would have invited her to this ceremony; as it was, her mother had taken her away and probably had already slapped the bejesus out of her. Melinda Pardo, who finished half a dozen strokes behind Vicki, attended the ceremony as runner-up.

Breann Claudeson, Yolanda Rivera's assistant, hosted the ceremony.

"Yolanda sends her regrets," Breann said. "She really wanted to be here on this special day, but she's in southern California, getting things ready for next week."

She introduced everyone she considered worthy of acknowledging. She ignored Helene and me.

Morrie Rosenthal presented Vicki with a huge replica of the winner's check for $300,000. The real check would travel from the sponsor to the LPGA to Vicki's checking account, because they always did it that way.

"Congratulations, sweetie," said the suave gentleman. "I'm sure this money will buy you all the blush-on and Tampax you'll need for a while. Har, har."

Vicki smiled and thanked everyone, especially Huey Tyler, the resort's head pro, who agreed to caddy for her on virtually no notice. "Huey has also agreed to resign his position here and go to California with me next week and be my caddy again. Wish us luck!" She pointed at him and he waved at the crowd.

Breann Claudeson introduced Can't Swim and invited him to say a few words, since he was one of the "top dogs" of the entire resort.

At the microphone, Can't Swim said, "May the winds blow strong and true to make your tee shots land on the green…may the rains wait for you to finish your day's golf."

As soon as he sat, Always Stoned got up and went to speak. "May the sun and the rains make for a good harvest of cannabis to make us feel good, yeah…and may the white girls walk around naked to get their supple young breasts nice and tan, oh yeah—"

Just then Newt Hoyle shoved Always Stoned away from the microphone. He told the man to go back to his seat, sit down and take s nap.

Newt said, "I'm available to do business if anyone wants to talk about buying a home site." Then he talked about a battle that had happened directly underfoot many years earlier. "We have a little something special for you right now. two of our locals, Raised by Snakes and Never Bathes, are going to perform a song about that battle."

I immediately tuned them out and, after a respectable amount of time, Helene and I caught up with Vicki and the three of us took off.

Helene said, "California, here we come…again."

I said, "Goodbye and good riddance, New Mexico."

PART THREE

SHE'S OUT OF MY LEAGUE

29

"This is nice," I said, sitting directly across from Helene. "It's so much fun hanging out with you."

"Well, I just couldn't stand the idea of going from Sussudio to Albuquerque to Los Angeles, or whatever our route would be." Helene shuddered. "Those airports! All that waiting!"

"Yeah! Fuck that!" We both laughed.

So Helene had decided to spend some of Vicki's winnings on chartering a Learjet to take us from Sussudio's local airport to Palm Springs. The aircraft, small and plush, could seat nine but carried only the Vachon ladies, Huey Clegg, Kit Manley, Melinda Pardo and myself. Helene thought it would make for good politics to give Kit and Melinda a ride.

Helene nodded. "This is the way to go. A brief, comfy flight. Eat a sandwich, read a magazine, take a nap and you're there. But maybe I shouldn't have spent so much money on this charter."

"You both deserve it. Anyway, Tiger Woods charters a flight just to go to the washroom."

We said nothing more for a few minutes. Then I leaned over towards her and said, "We've known each other for damn close to a couple of weeks now, yes?"

She nodded.

"Which means you've had a bit of time to get comfortable with me, yes?"

She nodded again.

"So, what would you say if I asked you out on a date?"

She puckered her lips a bit. "A *date*?"

"Yeah. Like we get dressed up. We do dinner and dancing. I light your smokes for you, except that smoking is illegal indoors, so maybe we'll have to go outside. But, you know, a date."

"You're taking a big risk here, Wasserman. Isn't it unethical for a reporter to date the mother of the person he's writing about?"

"We won't tell anyone. It'll be our little secret."

She chuckled. "Ooh, I like secrets." Then, "Yeah."

"What does 'yeah' mean?"

"It means"—she gave me a big, sweet, toothy

smile, the one I had seen a few times already light up her daughter's face—"Why, yes, Clancy, I would *love* to do dinner and dancing with you."

"That's more like it. We'll party down in Palm Springs."

I sat back and looked over at her. She was still smiling. I smiled, too.

Well done, Clancy.

We stayed at the Desert Dreams Hotel, the tournament's headquarters, just a few minutes from everything. They had booked me into the main building and Huey Tyler into the room next to mine. Vicki and her mum were staying in a cabana a dozen steps away from the hotel's huge swimming pool.

At the front desk, the clerk handed me a press kit for the Reboul Classic. The tournament's organizers had left it for me. In my room, I skimmed it and tossed it aside. I knew Palm Springs even if they called it something else, like Rancho Mirage or La Quinta. I had been here several times to cover the

Bob Hope Classic, which was basically just courses scattered about here and there, with a pressroom and some hotels and bars.

However, I had never been to Palm Springs at this particular time of the year, known by some as "Sappho in the Desert." The tournament had become an opportunity for friends of Gertrude S. to make out and grope each other in public, accidentally or deliberately freaking out the heterosexuals. I had been around long enough to know what was going on and when to look the other away.

For example, I knew enough not to go into a bar called Members Not Allowed and I made sure to stay out of a place called Girlfriends.

Lately, the week had come to belong to the moneyed lesbians who had spent their lives getting college degrees and building careers instead of cruising bars, getting high and shacking up. These women rented condos and houses and threw lavish parties whose main message was: You may have a problem with my sexuality, but I'm rich and successful and not above buying your friendship.

I feared that some of those non-males would be at

the tournament that week, the people who dressed for combat and wore tattoos of the gay pride flag with the words ONLY GOD CAN JUDGE ME.

I hoped those non-males would stay away from the swimming pool after we'd checked in. I didn't want them to see Helene and Vicki at the pool in their skimpy bikinis. Those tough dykes might kick my ass and fuck my women.

30

Tuesday, the night of my first date with Helene, arrived almost before I was prepared for it. She had said, "OK, all right, whatever," which I took to mean yes.

I looked out my window and observed a crowd of Occupy Palm Springs zealots yapping away outside the hotel's front doors. I probably would have been oblivious to them altogether if I hadn't decided to take a walk after spending the afternoon beating off to Internet porn videos.

The Occupy people had gathered to tell Palm Springs how wrong it was that this affluent community had so much while others had little or nothing.

I spoke to a Richard Ramirez lookalike as he walked in a circle with a couple of Angela Davises, a few Osamas one or two Kurt Cobains and a Joan Baez.

"I don't know why I'm here," the Night Stalker

told me. "I just saw this group of people waving signs and chanting, and I got drawn in by their energy."

I went up to an Angela Davis, who was wearing a hippie dress and sandals.

"I guess you have pretty strong feelings about this," I said.

"About what?" she asked.

"Laurent Reboul and his tournament."

She shook her head. "I don't know who Laurent Reboul is."

"Really? Then why are you out here demonstrating?" I asked her.

"Because," she said, "I hate golf."

"Why?"

"Because," she answered, "I'm a golf widow. My fucking girlfriend is addicted to that shit."

I have always had quite a disdain for protests. Most of the demonstrators I have seen seemed to be a ragtag bunch of welfare losers and assorted fuckups who had nothing better to do than rake the muck in front of the TV news cameras.

I've read Thoreau's essay about civil disobedience and watched footage of Mario Savio at Berkeley in 1964. I've wondered if such fun and games could have been stopped back then before public pissing and moaning became so popular. Maybe if the chancellor of UC-Berkeley had grown a pair and said, "Guess what, Mario! You and your pals can go home now *because you're all expelled!*"

Back when I was an undergraduate at Northup University in the 1980s, I knew that my American brothers and sisters in the 1960s were not protesting the Vietnam War and they did not especially give a rat's ass about free speech. What they *did* care about, very deeply, was staying out of the Army, staying in school, staying stoned and getting it on.

I go on YouTube sometimes and laugh out loud at the footage of the Vietnam War and draft dodgers. All those hippies waving signs saying MAKE LOVE, NOT WAR and BETTER RED THAN DEAD. I got the impression that none of them had the slightest idea of what was happening over there in Indochina, and they all wanted to remain ignorant and indignant.

Of course, when I studied at Northup, I looked forward to boozy, dopey, sexy weekends, but that meant a couple of days away from the hassles of school, not a lifestyle unto itself.

Back in college, a friend said to me, "Look, Clancy, when you get high or tap some girl's ass, you don't feel aggressive afterwards, right? Well, lots of sex and drugs for everyone—that's a solution to the world's problems."

I said, "But wait a minute. The men's erections will quit happening over time, and then what will you have? Just a bunch of stoners with no motivation to make the world a better place. Human advancement will cease, and nobody will be inventing the cool shit we all like to waste our money on."

But there are people who were born to protest and demonstrate. Those events usually happen outdoors, in good weather. Some folks love to get out there and work on their suntans while they rage against the machine.

The restaurant I chose for our date was Guido Sarducci's, in downtown Palm Springs, a short walk from our hotel. I had been there a couple of times and had gone there originally because people had told me that Frank Sinatra and Canadian zillionaire Jimmy Pattison loved the place. I liked it, too—the place, dark and cool, was full of brass, glass and dark wood. The meat sauce smelled and tasted homemade.

I hoped that it had changed very little or not at all. Up in Bayporte, stingy, greedy new proprietors had taken over good old restaurants and destroyed them with things like cheaper ingredients and smaller portions.

I knocked on the door of the cabana, it swung open and Vicki stood before me in a skintight T-shirt and short shorts.

"Wow! Mum, check this out!" Vicki called to her mother. "Your hot date is here!"

I had put on my only dark-blue suit and partnered it with a black T-shirt and burgundy shoes. It didn't really seem like the most appropriate outfit for a fifty-year-old man, but if anyone didn't like it, fuck 'em.

"Better hurry, Mum," Vicki was saying. "If you don't get out here soon, I may steal him for myself."

"Thank you, Vicki," I said.

"No problem, Clancy," she said with a giggle.

"So," I said, "how do you like the golf course so far?"

She shrugged. "It's better than the last couple, but that isn't saying much. Par is probably a good score on this one. Ask me again later, after I've had some more experience with it."

"How's your backside?"

She slapped it hard. "Pain is all gone."

"Nice. What are you doing tonight?"

"I have a big date with the TV set. MTV is running a *Jackass* marathon."

Just then Helene appeared in black jeans, a black silk T-shirt and black boots. I suddenly felt weak everywhere and for a moment thought I would need to sit.

She had her hair down, and it tumbled about her shoulders the way a model's did in a shampoo commercial.

"Shall I go to the printer's and have the invites

made up now?" I asked, my pulse racing and the butterflies in my stomach slamming into each other.

"Do you always use such tacky lines on your first date?" Helene retorted.

"What are you two yakking about?" asked Vicki.

"Just two adults acting like adolescents," Helene said.

I tried a different tack. "You look very beautiful tonight."

She smiled. "That's more like it. Let's go eat. I'm famished."

31

There's an old saying that goes, "Money talks and bullshit walks." That certainly was the case at Guido Sarducci's. Fortunately, my one-hundred-dollar bill told the maître d' exactly what he wanted to hear. As soon as I pressed the folded C-note into his palm he moved us from a rickety table by the washroom door to a booth in a quiet, intimate section of the restaurant. Our server even smiled at us.

They must have figured out that we were prepared to spend money, because our server, whose name sounded like Roseanne Roseannadanna, brought our drinks promptly: a double Canadian Comfort over ice for me and a glass of vintage white wine for Helene.

I had hoped our server might tell us some gossip about the rich and famous people who frequented this place, but no; she simply did her job and went off to look after her other guests.

I raised my glass to her; she raised hers to me.

"This," she said, "is one very expensive glass of wine. I really don't need it; I could have done with a glass of house wine."

"The Moet Chandon we'll have with dinner is even pricier than that. Drink it. Enjoy it. You only live once."

We clinked our glasses and drank.

"Did you see those Occupy people outside our hotel?" I asked her. "They made enough noise. We walked around the back of the hotel to avoid them."

She shook her head. "I spent the whole day by the pool. The room-service waiter said there was some kind of thing going on outside, but not to worry. It was just people demanding a new world order." Helene paused. "I'm not into protesting. If anything, I would protest against protesting. I am fanatical about not being a fanatic."

"I was a kid during the Summer of Love," I said. Of course, all that stuff—Vietnam, the draft, hippies—all seemed very American to me, very foreign, since I was a Canadian in Bayporte. The big social upheaval happening here in the States just didn't have any impact on us at all. It was like our prime minister said to their president, 'If you want to go into Vietnam and pick up where the French left off, you'll have to do it without us.'"

I nodded. "The same thing happened with Iraq and Desert Storm or Desert Shield, or whatever they called it. The Americans got really mad at us when Jean Chretien said he wouldn't send any Canadian troops over there because he figured it wasn't *our* problem."

"My parents sure didn't have much use for hippies, protestors and rabble rousers. My father was a businessman who wanted to maintain the status quo, and my mother didn't want any peaceniks blocking her way when she went shopping."

"Your mother would have been quite happy here in Palm Springs," I said.

"Oh, she's been here, and she *does* like it. She thinks Camel, Santa Barbara and La Jolla are pretty decent places, too."

"Those are all very affluent communities," I said. "You would never know that we were suffering through an economic downturn."

"Vicki and I aren't having any 'economic

downturn,' thanks to her winning the Go-4-It last week."

"Let's hope she keeps it up."

Helene smiled. "I hear that."

Our food arrived, and we dived in.

Helene devoured her Caesar salad so fast that I wondered if she'd had a chance to taste it. She took her time with her eight-ounce filet mignon with asparagus and closed her eyes as she savored her steak's wonderful succulence. I had oysters on schnitzel with a side of cabbage.

She had half a bottle of pricey white wine and I had two more double Canadian Comforts over ice.

As we ate, I told her some of the day's news. "Detroit declared bankruptcy today. Maybe Chicago will be next. This makes me think the mid-Sixties were a better time. Sure, Vietnam was about to happen, but the economy was robust and the unemployment rate was very low. There was no HIV and plenty of 'free love.' You didn't have to go to the

Haight-Ashbury to get it on."

Helene swallowed a mouthful of wine, licked her lips and inched closer to me. "You don't have to go to the Haight to get laid now, either. You can get some right here in Palm Springs."

I suddenly grew hot and flushed. My armpits felt flooded. She wasn't just flirting; she was making me a straight-ahead, no-bullshit offer. I caught the arm of our server as she swept by. I cleared my throat and reached for my wallet.

"Check, please."

32

Helene left my room in the middle of the night, sometime between two and three, but returned at breakfast time, minutes after Vicki had left for the golf course. We didn't have breakfast, or lunch, and neither of us felt hungry for food. By the early afternoon, tired and sweaty, we took a break from thrashing about between the soaked bedclothes and noticed that the CNN anchor had been watching us, probably for hours. Shame on the dirty bugger.

This, I said to myself, is love.

By and by we showered and made ourselves presentable for dinner with Vicki in one of the hotel's restaurants. Helene and I played it cool and pretended we hadn't spent the afternoon going at it like a couple of rabbits.

"Do you think she'll suspect anything?" Helene asked me.

"Yes. You have that look about you."

"What look?"

"The look that says, 'I've just had my brains balled out for the first time in a long while and right now the world is a pretty nice place.'"

She chuckled. "Oh, *that* look." She paused. "You have it, too."

"Do I? Well, we'll just pretend that we don't. Nobody has to know about our torrid, passionate lovemaking."

In the restaurant, moments after our drinks arrived, Vicki asked, "Did you two have a nice afternoon?"

"Sure did," Helene said. "How did you enjoy the *Jackass* marathon?"

She shrugged. "I'd seen them all before."

"How did you enjoy your day on the golf course?" Helene asked.

Vicki smirked. "Not as much as you enjoyed *your* afternoon in Clancy's room."

Helene's face went red. "Excuse me?"

"I'm OK with it, Mum," Vicki said. She made a face at me and said, in a manly growl, "Buddy, you better be using protection."

I laughed despite myself.

"Why are you laughing?" Helene asked, her eyes narrowing. "It's not a bit funny."

"I'm laughing because we were trying to pretend that what happened hadn't happened, but she figured it all out right away."

"Yeah," said Vicki, "no secrets here. We're all cool."

"Wrong," said Helene, her lips pursed.

"Why?" asked Vicki. "Why are you getting so hot?"

"Because this conversation is inappropriate and I want to talk about something else."

"OK, Mum." Vicki rolled her eyes. "Take a 'Lude or something. Lighten up."

"Let's talk about golf. How did it go today? You have to be ready for this one because I don't think there'll be any Winnie Baxter-style meltdowns happening this time."

Vicki nodded. "This is a harder course, but I'll rise to the challenge." She sighed. "So, we're talking golf this evening and not…other things. Is that how it is?"

"Damn straight," said the mum.

"So," I asked Vicki, "what will you need to win this one?"

She frowned a bit. "Hope the breeze is gentle and blowing in my direction. Hit my tee balls extra hard and stay out of the rough. In other words, the usual."

"So it's all in your hands, eh? Nobody else matters?"

Vicki nodded. "I'm all there is. There ain't no one else."

"That's a winner's attitude," I told her.

"Beauty sleep time," she said, getting up and stifling a yawn. "Wish me luck. See you in the morning, Mum."

Vicki blew past us as Helene made one of her indignant, embarrassed faces and stared at the tabletop for several long moments.

33

My jaw fell open as I saw Yolanda Rivera, the LPGA commissioner, *schmoozing* with the Occupiers and outside the gates of Hollywoodland. I asked the driver of the press shuttle to let me off right there. The late-morning sun warmed my bones on that Thursday morning, the first day of the Reboul Classic.

Helene and Vicki had gone to the course a couple of hours earlier, in a courtesy car provided by Reboul. They needed to be there well before Vicki's noontime tee time with Sandi Shaffer and Pam Mackey.

I didn't know how Helene felt on so little sleep, but I was wide awake and even exhilarated. I had learned that when I spent the night making wild, passionate love to a beautiful woman, I could get by on virtually no sleep.

Dozens of Occupiers stood in front of the golf course. Yolanda seemed in deep conversation with one of them, a young woman in a hippie dress. She held a handmade sign saying HONK IF YOU HATE CAPITALISM.

"Yolanda Rivera!" I exclaimed. "Lovely to see you here!"

"Why *wouldn't* I be here, Clancy?" she asked, her brow furrowing.

"Why are you talking to these people?" I asked.

"I'm trying to reason with these people. Their presence here is inappropriate, and I want them to leave." She shook her head. "I can't imagine what Laurent Reboul must think. This is his first time sponsoring an event in America, and look at this eyesore he gets!"

The Occupiers surrounded us, glowering at us as if Yolanda and I represented everything wrong in the world. They looked like a bunch from Central Casting: Arabs wearing caftans, hippies, beatniks with sunglasses and berets.

"Our numbers will only grow," said the hippie girl with the sign. "We will not go away."

"Why are you here? What do you want?" I asked her. "This is a golf tournament. Many people from far away have come for this."

"Golf is ridiculous," she said. "It's a bunch of rich people knocking little white balls into holes."

"What would you do with all these golf courses," asked Yolanda, "if you owned them?"

"I would build houses on them," said the hippie girl, "so that poor people would have somewhere to live."

"You," said Yolanda, "are a naïve and dumb individual. The only reason you're out here today is to be on TV. I'm sure you've noticed the cameras and reporters."

"Yes," said the hippie girl. "We want our message to be known all over the world, and those TV people will do just that. 'Golf Doesn't Matter.' That's a song I just wrote, and maybe I'll perform it today."

"Free live entertainment?" I said. "I'll have to stick around for that."

"I don't know who you are," she told me, "but let me ask you something. Do you know any homeless people?"

"Only the ones I step over on my way to work."

"Do you think people should eat out of garbage cans and dumpsters?"

"Is this a trick question?"

Yolanda Rivera said to the hippie lady, "All you're doing is preventing a group of women, professional golfers, from competing in a tournament. Think about that."

The hippie girl cackled. "You're breaking my heart. A bunch of grown women have devoted their lives to hitting balls into holes. Maybe they should stop playing children's games and do something useful, like volunteering at a crisis center or maybe trying to be better wives and mothers."

"I wonder if all the golfers have arrived yet," I said, looking around. One of the beatnik girls caught my eye. She smiled; I smiled back. Then she made an obscene finger gesture at me.

"Our new sponsor," Yolanda told the hippie girl, "is Mister Reboul. What could he do to make you happy and gain your approval?"

"He could use all of his resources to eradicate poverty and homeless in America, starting with donating this golf course to the poor people. He might even try living as a poor person, to see what it's like."

34

The bad surprises kept on coming. Helene and I stood by the first tee and saw the statue of Laurent Reboul standing in a bed of flowers. Yolanda Rivera had commissioned the statue as a gift for the French guy who had invested so much money in the tournament.

The statue of a handsome, swarthy man in a dark suit, light shirt and orange tie stood nearly a hundred feet in the air. His hands seemed a bit outstretched, as if challenging the Occupiers to a fight, and I couldn't really discern the expression on his face.

Helene and I looked it over as Yolanda Rivera and an unfamiliar man came up to us.

"What do you think of him?" Yolanda asked, pointing at the statue.

I shrugged. "Why does he look like plaster?"

"Because he is. We didn't have enough time to make a marble or bronze one. So we settled for plaster and paint."

"The main thing," I said, "is this: Does Reboul like it?"

"He doesn't think the statue is handsome enough."

"That figures," I muttered.

"Funny, Clancy. You make jokes, but Laurent was quite touched by this gesture, and we have assured him that we will have another statue made—of marble or bronze, whichever he likes—up and on display well before next year's Reboul Classic."

I extended my hand to the man standing next to Yolanda. He had a great tan and meticulous haircut. Whiter-than-white teeth.

"I'm Clancy Wasserman," I said.

He shook my hand. "Fred Cordoba."

"I've seen you before," I told him.

He smiled. "You certainly have. I've been in scores of movies. I do voiceovers, too. They call me "The most famous actor nobody knows," and they're right. I like it that way—the anonymity, the absence of death threats."

"And you golf, too, eh?"

"Not at all. But I love the courses themselves, the beauty of the land. You should come to my tent at the other end of the course. Good food and rink. Plus plenty of friendly people."

"More famous anonymous types?" I asked.

"That's funny!" Fred said, without laughing.

Yolanda perused the statue and said, "We had thought about putting a dog up there with him, but decided it should be about Laurent only. Plus, we're trying to make people forget that he's made much of his money selling horse meat as dog food."

"Good thinking," said Helene.

"Not to be rude," I said, "but Helene and I have to go now and watch some golf."

Helene and I stood side by side and bowed our heads as Vicki had the worst afternoon of her young golfing life. She shot an abysmal 88 and at times, shaking with frustration, nearly bent her putter over her thigh.

Vicki finished her day with a huge bogey—five over par—that left her in a tie for 25th place. Cristie

Kerr led the Reboul Classic with an even-par 80.

Vicki had no catastrophic moments during the afternoon. She mostly just overhit or underhit her tee balls, then had a bit more trouble than usual getting into putting range. Once there, she missed a few tap-ins she would have made on any other day.

Helene and I spoke to Huey Clegg just after Vicki had skulked into the scorer's tent.

"She got off to a bad start," he said. "When she made par on the first two holes, Sonja Sommers birdied both of them, and Vicki got this *attitude* going and she couldn't get her confidence back. Things got worse as Sonia got off to a lead and Vicki started trying to play catch-up instead of doing her own thing."

"I hope she doesn't blame you for any of this," said Helene.

Huey shook his head. "She's just pissed at herself. She'll get over it. She's young, tough and resilient." He sighed. "It's just been a shitty day in paradise."

A few moments later, Vicki, jaws and fists clenched, stomped out of the scorer's tent.

"I made half a dozen screw-ups out here today and

it *sucked*. It absolutely *sucked*." She took a long, anxious breath and blew it out. "How about that fourteenth hole? It's as flat as a pancake and slow as molasses. I've got an easy two-foot putt for par, right? So what happens? I miss it! Twice!"

"Vicki," said her mum, "don't get so upset. This is day one. You have plenty of more golf to be played. Tomorrow will be better."

I said, "It's been a difficult first day, Vicki, but I was expecting that. This was also your first time here, and that makes it even worse. So now you've had a chance to check it out here and see what you're up against. I know you feel really crappy about it at the moment, but you'll have more confidence tomorrow."

Vicki's lips stayed tight with anger. "Do you know how many times I went under par today? Zero! How retarded was that? Did you see my first putt on the eighth? A twelve-footer that rolled right past the hole by ten feet! Who was that clumsy bitch out there? It sure as hell wasn't Vicki Vachon."

"You weren't a 'clumsy bitch,' you were a golfer trying to catch up with Sonja Sommers," I told her.

"Maybe. But that's just the way I am. I usually get out to an early lead, but when someone else gets the lead, I'm like, 'I better get really aggressive and show my opponent who's boss.' Dammit! I'm gonna go practice some more. You two can go now. don't wait up for me. I've got to work off some of my anger."

She stormed off, her fists still clenched.

Helene sat back at a shaded table and chain-smoked Player's Lights while I went into the pressroom. Since the Reboul Classic was a major tournament, more reporters had arrived to cover the event, and I had to elbow my way into the pressroom. At least the Hottie and Go-4-It Classics, minor tournaments regarded with indifference by most of the sports world, had underpopulated pressrooms.

I stood and visited with a couple of friends: Ronny Cyrus from *Golfer's World* and Barry Smokewood, an editor at Outdoorsman Publications.

The three of us talked about how we were all cheering for a heterosexual woman to win the Reboul

Classic.

Miles O'Connell, the architect, sat in the interview section of the pressroom, explaining how he had not just improved but *changed* American golf through rebuilding and reshaping existing courses and bringing his magical touch to courses that, a year earlier, had been nothing but grass and trees.

I saw no rolling, skeptical eyes in the faces of the reporters recording his words. I perceived utter seriousness and sincerity in the face and voice of Miles O'Connell.

Soon I went back to join Helene. We agreed that it had been a sad day indeed for people who, like us, were fans of Vicki Vachon.

"Vicki kept on about the six mistakes she made," Helene pointed out. "But it was more than that. You saw the scorecard. It's the *elite* of women's golf she's playing against, and she's so far behind right now. Sonja, Annika, Suzanne, Lorena—Jesus, they're all here, and she's going to have to beat them! How will she do that?"

"By playing better," I said.

"No fuckin' shit," Helene muttered.

"Madam, such language," I muttered back. Then, "On the bright side, Winnie Baxter shot a seventy-eight. Inderjit Dhaliwal shot an eighty-seven."

"Too bad Inderjit didn't shoot an eighty-eight."

"Why?" I asked. "What's the difference between eighty-seven and eighty-eight?"

"There's all the difference in the world out here. If she had shot an eighty-eight, she would have been disqualified immediately. It's the LPGA's way of saying, 'If you can't do better than that, you shouldn't be here. So go home.'"

I nodded. "Good rule. This is a hard course. Maybe tomorrow Inderjit will have a bad day and be sent home."

Helene smiled. "Let's hope so."

35

Helene and I slept together but didn't do much. We made out, groped each other and moaned and groaned. We thought about doing more, but fell asleep in each other's arms and dreamed about life, death, marriage, divorce, love and hate.

Actually, we dreamed mostly about golf.

Helene hurried off to her cabana at around dawn so Vicki, upon awakening, would think her mum had spent the night there instead of with me. We met in the coffee shop for breakfast and ate in silence. Vicki had brought her iPad and tapped away on it as she shoveled forkfuls of scrambled eggs and potatoes into her mouth.

I looked up as I heard her groan.

"Something wrong?" Helene asked.

"The *Los Angeles Times*. 'The Hollywoodland course just gave teen queen from Canada a megadose of modesty and humility in the first round...'"

The three of us got a ride from a very old lady volunteer who had a man's gold Rolex and a diamond ring on every finger. Her skin was chocolate bronze

"I had never heard of Hollywoodland golf course until a little while ago," she told us. "It's just not exclusive enough for me. Would you look at all those people with their signs? What are they up to?"

As she tapped on the accelerator so the car would inch through the narrow pathway the police had provided, the driver looked at the tableau of scowling faces and hands slapping the windshield.

"Do you think the cops would mind," she asked us, "if I hit the gas and took out a few of these bums?"

"She should run for mayor," I muttered to Helene.

"She would win," Helene muttered back.

Right away, Helene and I perused the huge scoreboard that stood near the statue of Laurent Reboul. We wanted to see if the early starters were having success playing this course. No; all the ladies were over par.

Vicki had gone over to hit balls in the practice area even though her tee time was a few hours away.

Helene beamed as she gazed upon the scoreboard and saw that Inderjit Dhaliwal had shot a dreadful 45 over the first nine holes.

"Come on," she said, grabbing my arm. "Let's go check her out. We have plenty of time."

"Why do you want to watch Inderjit play?"

"So I can cough or fart on her backswing and mess up her concentration."

"You're above that sort of behavior," I said. "Aren't you?"

But we were already walking in Inderjit's direction.

"I'm supposed to be above that sort of behavior, eh?" Helene asked. "Well, what about when Inderjit tried to poison my daughter? Or when she kicked Vicki? Hey? And what does anybody do about it? They do dick. I've contacted Yolanda Rivera about it and all I get from her is a lot of air. 'We're checking it out' or 'We'll put it on our agenda' or 'We will need further proof that some wrongdoing has occurred.'" Helene shook her head and blew out a big breath.

"That Yolanda! Some commissioner, eh?"

"Do you know if Vicki has talked to the other golfers about Inderjit and Winnie?"

"Oh, I'm sure she hasn't. That's not her style. She just wants to pretend the ugly situation isn't there, so she can stay focused, win the damn thing and move on to the next one."

"But you're her mum and you feel that you have a responsibility to protect her from whatever or whoever tries to harm her."

"Bloody well right. So if the skinny Punjab gets close to shooting eighty-eight and I'm nearby—"

"I'll plug my ears and close my eyes."

We encountered Inderjit on the fifteenth hole.

"Mary Pickford was a Canadian," I told Helene.

"That right, eh?"

"Many celebrities have come from Canada."

"That's because Canada has so much fish, cattle and produce," Helene said. "Plus fresh air. It nourishes the brain."

"If Canada is such a fine place," I asked, "how come all its famous people move down to the States?"

"Because Canada is boring," she said.

"That's not a very nice thing to say about your home and native land."

"Native land, yes. But we own that place in Florida, and that's sort of our home. We now spend most of our time in this country, and we may both take out American citizenship eventually. Or at least Vicki will, if her fame and fortune continue."

"Which will probably happen," I said.

Helene shrugged.

We stood and watched Inderjit, who had been paired with Midori Suzuki, a Japanese girl who spoke no English and had no discernable golfing skills.

Inderjit, now a dozen over par, had ended up in the rough at fourteen.

I smiled with satisfaction that Inderjit and her ball were at the other side of the fairway from us, and out of earshot.

I watched Helene quiver with giggles as she watched Inderjit hack and chop at her ball.

"The poor thing," Helene said. "She obviously is quite mystified as to how to get out of the rough."

"She's going to end up with a double bogey," I said. And Inderjit did just that.

"But she's not done yet," Helene said. "She can get another bogey and a couple of cars and they won't kick her off the tour and send her back to India."

Helene let out a loud whimper when Inderjit sank a thirty-foot putt—a total fluke, of course, but it counted—after landing in the rough again on the sixteenth hole.

Next, at the par-four seventeenth, Helene whimpered some more as Inderjit sank a twenty-five-footer after goofing around in the rough some more.

"She is really starting to piss me off," Helene muttered.

But a few minutes later, we watched with fascination as Inderjit stood at her tee ball with her legs bent like a baseball hitter—who told her to do *that?*—and whacked her ball into the heavens. We watched it sail off in the direction of Cordoba's hospitality tent.

I thought: That tall, skinny Indian girl is a hell of a

lot stronger than she looks.

Helene gushed, "She's gone out of bounds, Clancy! I love it! Don't you love it?"

"Not as much as you do," I said.

We watched as the ball hit Cordoba's patio and bounce around before someone slapped it away. Helene threw back her head and cried out, "*Yeah, baby!*"

"Cheer up, Helene," I said.

"Isn't this fun? Come on, Clancy, let's go over there and console the dear girl. Maybe I can be the first to tell her she has to go home."

36

Helene simply glowed with joy as Inderjit finished
with a score of 91.

I said, "Helene, do you always find this much joy
in other people's hard luck?"

She giggled some more. Then Inderjit Dhaliwal
came moping out of the scorer's tent and over to us.

"They are telling me that my playing was so bad
that I am not permitted to be playing more," she said.

"It's worse than you think it is," Helene told her.

Inderjit frowned. "I am not understanding you."

Helene explained the eighty-eight rule. Tears
started streaming down Inderjit's pretty brown face.

"So I am not being able to play here for one year
and I am having to go through the qualifying again?"
She wiped away her tears and shed some more. "This
is too bad! I am having to stop playing golf in the
States!"

"Yes. You must go home to New Delhi, or wherever you came from. After what you and Winnie Baxter did to my daughter, I am happy you will be flying away very soon."

"I was not doing anything to her! Winnie was not harming her!"

"You know that's wrong. You know you did wrong," said Helene.

"No, please! I was meaning no harm. I was just playing tricks."

Inderjit started weeping again, and I very nearly felt badly for her. But I didn't. I wanted her to go back to India and was about to offer her a ride to the airport.

"Do you know what you did?" Helene asked her. "You put poison in my daughter's food. Then you run up from behind and *kick* her so that maybe you can *injure* her enough so Winnie Baxter can win the tournament. Don't deny one fucking word of it."

Inderjit wiped away the last of her tears and furrowed her brow. "How are you knowing these things?"

"I know these things because I have a brain and

can think. Now look, Inderjit: I want you to tell me the truth about what happened. Understand?"

"Are you being able to do something for me?" Inderjit asked, brightening up a bit. "You can be helping me to stay in States?"

"Could be."

I tried to make eye contact with Helene and shake my head a little, to discourage her from offering the kid things we couldn't deliver. But Helene just kept looking at Inderjit.

"If I am to be telling truth," Inderjit said, "you are helping me to be staying here and playing golf?"

"Talk to me. If I believe what you say, I will do what I can for you," said Helene.

Inderjit nodded and closed her eyes. "Winnie? She is not doing anything bad. She is not knowing about any of this."

"You did these things all by yourself? Without Winnie's knowledge or assistance?"

"Yes, mum. Acting all by myself."

Helene sneered. "Bullshit."

"I am saying what is true. I am never wanting to harm Vicki, just wanting to scare her."

"You know that shit you put in her food? It could have been fatal."

"No, mum, I only use enough to make her start feeling ill."

"How did you know how much or little to use?"

"Because I am knowing about these things." Inderjit crossed her arms over her chest. "I have done a bad thing, and I am feeling sorry. I am doing it to Vicki only for the money."

"You got *paid* to poison Vicki?" Helene asked, incredulous.

"Yes, mum. I am poor Indian girl wanting better life in States, so I am accepting money to harm Vicki."

"You're such a dumb-ass," muttered Helene. "Who paid you? Winnie?"

"No, her mother."

Helene's jaw dropped. *"Dawn Baxter?"*

Inderjit nodded.

Helene took a deep breath, gave a disgusted shake of her head and looked at me. "Did you just hear what I just heard?"

"'Fraid so."

"How much did Dawn pay you?" Helene asked Inderjit.

"Three thousand dollars."

"Dawn Baxter paid you three thousand dollars to attack Vicki. That's your story, eh?"

Inderjit nodded. "I am poor Indian girl with no pot to pee in. I am needing money for Hottie jeans and Cover Girl makeup."

"Let's go," Helene said, grabbing Inderjit's hand.

"Where are you wanting me to go?"

"To see the wonderful wizard of Oz. Where the fuck do you *think* I'm taking you? To the LPGA tent so that you can tell them what you've just told me and sign a written version of what you've said." She motioned to me. "You come too, Clancy. Maybe with a media member with us, they won't blow us off quite so fast."

"I'm with ya, boss," I said.

"Why I am having to do this?" Inderjit pouted.

"Why? Because if you don't do as I say, I'll wring your fucking neck. Good enough reason?"

"Ow! You're hurting me!" Inderjit cried out as Helene half-dragged the girl by the hand.

37

We knocked once on the door of the LPGA office and pushed it open before anyone inside could invite us inside. I sat in a corner and watched as Helene pushed Inderjit into a seat across the desk from Breann Claudeson, Yolanda Rivera's second-in-command. Helene ordered Inderjit to spill it.

Breann did much frowning and shrugging. "Poisoning incident six months ago? You assaulted Vicki Vachon in New Mexico last week? This is the first I've heard of it," she said. "Nobody told me that Dawn Baxter slapped Winnie at the Cover Girl."

Breann tapped her pencil on her desktop and narrowed her eyes. I grinned, believing that, like all Number Twos, she wanted to be Number One. She was probably thinking, 'How can I use this information to force Yolanda into resigning so that *I* can be the boss?'

She got up, went to her door and and Inderjit, said

in a loud voice, "Go get Dawn Baxter and bring her to me immediately. I think she's in Fred Cordoba's tent. Then find Yolanda and send her, too."

She went back to her desk and sat down. "Helene, what do you want us to do about what Inderjit has told us? Press charges?"

Helene shook her head. "Not just yet. I thought Winnie and Inderjit were the culpable parties, but now I'm sure it was Dawn. Winnie had nothing to do with it, and Inderjit doesn't even know what she doesn't know. I have something in mind that Yolanda may agree to, because I know how she hates scandals and bad press."

Breann gave her a grim little smile. "Don't we all."

"Here's the deal. Inderjit will sit here and write a confession in English, stating what she did and who paid her. In return for her cooperation, we will say that she did not submit a score of eight-eight or over. Instead, she withdrew; but because she did not know how to withdraw, she didn't do it officially. You or another LPGA official will alter her scorecard to read eighty-seven, and she will be free to play golf here."

"And if I say no, I have a feeling that Clancy

Wasserman here will write all about it in *Canadian Sports* magazine. Is that why you brought him here?"

"Absolutely," said Helene.

"What's to stop him from writing about it anyway?"

I grinned. "I'll do whatever Helene wants me to do."

Breann Claudeson gave Inderjit several sheets of lined paper and a ballpoint pen. "Write it all down. If you need help with spelling or grammar, just say so." To an office flunky she said, "Go to the scorer's tent and bring me the last two dozen scorecards from those women who have finished their rounds. I want to have a look at them just to make sure that everything's in order."

To us, Breann asked, "Does anyone want anything to drink?"

Inderjit and I said no. Helene said, "A cup of iced tea would be all right, but I would *love* a cigarette."

Breann reached into her pocket and pulled out a package of Newports.

"You smoke?" Helene asked, wide-eyed with surprise.

"I'm trying to quit," Breann replied, putting one cigarette into her mouth, lighting it, then handing the package and lighter to Helene.

"Quitting is easy," said Helene, lighting up. "I've done it a hundred times."

Inderjit looked up at them, scowling. "Why are you smoking? This is very bad. Very, very bad."

Helene took a long, deep drag and exhaled in the girl's direction. "How come you're not writing?"

The two smokers took turns tapping their cigarettes on the glass ashtray between them. "What do you want us to do about Dawn Baxter?" Breann asked.

"Bar her from the tour indefinitely. I'll go before the board, if it comes down to that."

Breann blew out a cloud of smoke and said, "I can't believe Yolanda withheld this matter from me. She rarely tells me *anything*."

"Totally unacceptable. Not very professional of her…and that's coming from the mother of *Vicki Vachon*."

"I hear that. We don't want to get on your bad side."

Just then Breann's flunky came in with the stack of scorecards Breann wanted. Then she stood there, open-mouthed and staring, at the sight of her boss and Vicki Vachon's mother smoking in the office.

Breanne blew out some smoke and asked, "Is there a problem?"

The flunky shook her head.

"Then get back to work," the deputy commissioner ordered.

The flunky nodded and walked out the door.

Claudia flipped through the scorecards and in a moment found Inderjit Dhaliwal's. "Must do this carefully," she said, twirling her pencil between her fingers. She erased the 91 and wrote WD in its place.

"I am not here," I said. "I am not aware of what is happening, and nobody has smoked a cigarette."

Inderjit Dhaliwal finished writing her confession and handed it to Breann, who read through it, nodded and put it into her photocopier. She handed one copy to Helene, who folded the document and slipped it into her shoulder bag.

Presently Dawn Baxter entered the office, snarling at the security guard behind her as if he'd just pinched her ass.

"You want something with me?" she asked.

"Yes, Dawn. Read this," said Breann, handing her a copy of the confession.

Dawn Baxter moved her lips as she read. She furrowed her brow and swallowed hard. Then she laughed as she handed the sheet of paper back to Breann.

"Didn't think we would ever catch you, eh?" Helene asked.

Dawn glowered at Helene. "Are you behind this, Helene? What's in it for her? Did you pay Inderjit to write this?"

"That's funny, Dawn," Helene said. "But you're busted."

Dawn looked over at Breann. "Are you going to believe what Inderjit wrote? She's just a sniveling little bitch from India."

"I'm going to call for an emergency meeting of the LPGA's board of directors as soon as the Reboul Classic is over. Then we'll deal with it.

"You will receive a request to appear, and you may bring an attorney. We believe that this matter is between you and us; your daughter is in no way involved. Miz Vachon does not wish to press charges, but she does want you barred from the tour and maybe she will seek to get a restraining order against you."

"A restraining order?" Dawn Baxter asked. "What the hell for?"

"So you won't try to kill my daughter again, you evil cunt," Helene told her.

Dawn Baxter made a wheezing sound, as if she'd just been punched in the solar plexus. Then she straightened her back and said, "I refuse to listen to any more of this bullshit." She walked out, and a minute or two later, Hope Moniquez, the LPGA official in charge of player interviews, came in.

"Breann," she said, "have you been looking for Yolanda?"

"I certainly have. Where is she?"

"She's in Amsterdam."

Breann's jaw dropped open. "This is the Reboul Classic! A major event for us here, and our commissioner has flown off to Europe? When? Why?"

"She left last night. She said there was a conference she wanted to attend. I guess she assumed you would be here to mind the store."

Breann shook her head in disbelief. "But she didn't bother to tell *me* about her absence?"

Hope shrugged. "Yolanda's like that sometimes, you know."

Hope left the office. Helene and Breann, after staring at each other for a moment, burst out with nervous laughter. "Yolanda, the commissioner, flew away at this crucial time because she thought she would have more fun in Europe."

"Maybe," said Helene, "you should bring this up during one of your LPGA meetings."

"Yes, ma'am," said the second-in-command.

Helene and I stood out in the sunshine and watched as Vicki worked on a 74.

"'Sorry, but the commissioner isn't here. She's off

in Europe, checking out some conference.'" Helene let loose a belly laugh.

"You like that, eh?" I asked.

"Like it? I fuckin' love it. I'll never forget it. I'll save it for when I'm feeling down and it'll pick me right back up."

"I love it when you laugh." I especially loved it when she could smile and be happy as we watched Vicki make bad tee shots and struggle with her putts.

Helene studied the scoresheet and groaned. "Angela Stanford leads this thing by several strokes. Vicki is tied for ninth, but Kit Manley, Cristie Kerr, Annika Sorenstam…they're all ahead of her. We're fucked."

"Maybe not. This course is one tough son of a bitch. They're all struggling. Plus, she's now ninth, which is much better than being twentieth, which she was yesterday."

"I don't know if her performance here is going to help your story about her," Helene said.

"It's not about this, it's about her," I said. "You know, 'Canadian girl makes good in America.' Our readers really get off on that kind of stuff."

"Will she still make the cover of *CS* if she finishes in ninth place?"

I shrugged. "I don't know, Helene. My boss makes those decisions. This is March; who else can he put on the cover? Some NHL guy with a thrice-broken nose and no front teeth? I think Vicki on the over would sell many more copies, especially if she isn't wearing very much."

<u>38</u>

We sat down with Vicki and told her all about Dawn Wendell and her plot. "So Dawn and Winnie have gone away now, hey? And she paid only that much? What an insult. I thought I'd be worth more."

The three of us sat in their cabana just before dinnertime. Helene and I told Vicki about of what had happened that afternoon. We omitted that nasty business about altering Inderjit Dhaliwal's scorecard. Some things just seemed better left unsaid.

"You can't talk about any of this to anyone," Helene admonished Vicki. "Not even Huey."

Vicki nodded. "I'm glad Winnie didn't get into any trouble. She really is a decent person and a good friend. I knew she wouldn't try to maim me."

Helene said, "I overreacted. I need to apologize to Winnie."

Soon we went into the hotel's dining room, where Huey Clegg sat waiting for us. We all took our seats, and Vicki, looking around the room, spotted Winnie Baxter sitting alone. Vicki caught her eye, motioned for her to sit with us. Winnie nodded, got up and came bounding over to us, all smiles.

The two girls sat side by side, and I observed how different they were. Vicki, tall and blonde, with a peaches-and-cream complexion, made Winnie look mousy and meaningless. Winnie's eyes darted about the faces surrounding us, as if seeking cues as to what do say and do. Winnie, a year older than Vicki, looked like the younger girl's clueless kid sister.

"My mother has a migraine and is lying down in our room," Winnie explained. "Inderjit withdrew today because of a sore wrist or something and she's upstairs watching TV. I barely made the cut, you know, but I'm hoping to do better tomorrow and leave this place with a decent check in my pocket."

She turned to Vicki and added, "You can win this thing. I'm sure of it."

"I guess. But I really have to play great tomorrow. Nothing was easy out there today, and I kept missing on putts I should have sunk. I got caught in the rough, too, and that's just not *me*." She brightened up.

"But, yeah, I'll do better tomorrow. And if that Angela Stanford starts to choke, well, I'll really mow her down."

Everybody laughed.

On Saturday, more people showed up to watch the tournament, and so did the TV crews. Many of the spectators were nonmales with short hair, sunglasses, tank tops and cargo pants. I supposed they were cheering mostly for Kit Manley; if I had been one of them, I would have wanted Kit to win. But I wondered: Did a woman like Vicki, in many ways still a girl and in all ways the most feminine of females, appeal to these diesel dykes? I shuddered at the notion.

The Occupiers had pretty much moved on; I saw only a dozen or so, and they stood in a circle, muttering to each other.

Vicki had a better day, shooting an even 70. Nikki Garrett, her partner that day, finished with an identical score. But Michelle Wie turned in a 70 and moved into a first-place tie with Angela Stanford. By late afternoon, Vicki ended up in fifth place, behind a veritable who's-who of golf: Angela Stanford, Michelle Wie, Annika Sorenstam, Paula Creamer.

Before I went to Vicki and Helene's cabana for a room-service dinner, I got a call from Newt Hoyle in Sussudio.

"Boy," he said, "I've got a couple of fellas out here playing golf, and they want to gimme some action on that girlie-girl thing you're covering right now. That Canuck cutie with the big titties, is she still there?"

"Vicki? Yeah, she's still here," I said.

"She playing good?"

"Good enough."

He snorted. "Well, shit, what the fuck's that mean? I ain't got Alzheimer's yet, you know. I need info. She's in fifth place right now. What I need to know is: Will she win it? Talk to me."

"She says she's gonna win it."

"Alrighty, then. I'm gonna go ahead and make that bed. Vicki says she's gonna win, then it must be so."

We ate mostly in silence. Vicki devoured her chicken pasta dish, then said goodnight and slipped into her bedroom to let TV music videos bore her to sleep. I could tell that her mind was racing with thoughts of the next day's golfing. Often, the most difficult challenge a golfer faces while competing is to concentrate, live in the here and now, and ignore all the distractions that buzz around her. But I didn't say anything to her. I knew she already knew it.

Helene and I went to the bar. I had a Diefenbaker beer and Helene had a glass of Canadian sparkling cider. We sat outside so she could smoke.

"Quite a daughter you have there," I said, feeling the compulsion to speak. I couldn't think of anything to add, so I just nodded, to add emphasis.

We fell silent again, and I smiled.

"What's funny?" she asked.

"Nothing."

"Yes," she said. "You were smiling about something. Tell me."

"I was just thinking," I said. "I've been a reporter for years now, and in the past little while I've done everything an ethical journalist shouldn't do."

"Like what?"

"Oh, cheering on one player, screwing her mother, feeling satisfied that her opponents are getting into trouble. Journalism professors always emphasize objectivity, because that's what makes journalism a fine institution. It refuses to be corrupted. If you're a journalist, you report the facts, not your opinion, and you certainly don't try to promote a girl golfer's career just because you're having a personal relationship with her mum."

"And you've compromised your integrity this time?" she asked.

I nodded.

"Well," Helene added, "what are you going to do about it?"

I smirked. "I'm going to have another drink."

40

As a journalist, I have heard many people say, "I was supposed to be on the plane that went down," or, "I was late getting to work at the World Trade Center, so I wasn't there when the planes crashed into the towers." I've read a hundred more stories about people who, for reasons they will never understand, have avoided catastrophes.

I have never had such an experience, but at Hollywoodland that Sunday morning, if I had been near the wrong place at the wrong time, I could have said forever after, "That statue of Laurent Reboul came this close to falling on me."

Actually, it didn't fall; the Occupiers pushed it over. They bought tickets and went in just to attack the statue, perhaps having surmised that Laurent Reboul represented everything bad, corrupt and ugly in the world, and since fucking over the actual man would be impossible or at least legally unwise, vandalizing the plaster man would have to do.

Helene and I arrived less than an hour after the incident. Breann Claudeson greeted us, holding one section of plaster arm.

"As you can see, we're having some getting him righted and fastened in there. They broke off part of an arm, but I think we can get it repaired.

"Poor Dawn Baxter and Laurent!" Breann closed her eyes and shook her head for a moment. "I was standing nearby while the troublemakers did it. The statue hit Dawn and Laurent. They were both sort of spacing out, so they didn't even see it hit them. Dawn got a broken shoulder and Laurent was knocked unconscious. He was still unresponsive when the paramedics took him away. I hope he doesn't die or anything."

"Maybe he'll change his mind about the Reboul Classic and pull out," said Helene.

"That would thrill everyone except Yolanda Rivera," I said. We all laughed.

"I got a golf cart," Breann told us, "and went as fast as I could to the practice area so I could tell Winnie what had just happened to her mother and if she wanted to withdraw and go see Dawn in the hospital. Winnie asked, 'Is she going to die?' and I said, 'Eventually, but not today.' So she said, 'I'm going to keep practicing. Tell her I'll be up to see her soon. She would want me to do well today.' "

Every nonmale in southern California seemed to come to the Reboul Classic on Sunday, their sleeveless T-shirts exposing forests of armpit hair. They hooted, whistled and cheered for certain golfers more than others, and I knew they were all sweet on Kit Manley.

"Kit's paired with Vicki today," Helene said. "I hope Vicki doesn't get freaked if she starts getting attention from Kit's fans."

"Not to worry," I said. "It's when she gets *no* attention from Kit's fans that she needs to get nervous."

Since the Reboul Classic was in California, they needed to start early so the day's play would be over by the time the TV news aired in the east.

I had no deadline at all. My piece on Vicki Vachon, a feature story known to my *CS* colleagues as "Tee & A," would be done when I declared it so. If Kerry, my boss, had an issue with that, too bad.

Helene and I waited at the first tee for the golfers to come out. Soon the *CS* photographer found us. A tall, swarthy man laden with equipment, he came up to me and said, "I need to see your identity papers."

"But Officer," I said, offering him my wrists to handcuff, "I'm just waiting here for a friend. You gonna bust me for nothin', man?"

We both laughed hard and shook hands. He was Dieter Schloss, who'd had years of experience working for European publications before moving to Canada and working for us.

"This is Vicki Vachon's mum," I said to him. "You'll want to get her picture, too—for obvious reasons."

Dieter nodded. "I just got in from Los Angeles, where I was shooting the Clippers. They weren't very friendly, but no team today is friendly towards the media. I guess they've stuck too many needles in their asses."

"I guess."

Dieter circled Helene, squinting into his viewfinder, catching her from every angle. She frowned, looked away, smiled, then struck a couple of cheesecake poses and, finally, looked into the distance with a look of alarm, as if her girl were out there trying to sink a difficult putt.

"I've got the mum, so where's her foxy daughter?" Dieter asked. "I don't have much time. Kerry wants me in Oakland tonight to shoot the Raptors versus the Warriors."

"The 'foxy daughter,'" Helene interjected, "is over there. She's wearing a very short dark skirt, a white blouse, a white cap. She has blonde hair, pretty titties and a stupid onion." She turned to me, smirking. "Isn't that how you guys describe her when she's not around?"

"Yes, ma'am." Dieter nodded and hurried off to join the other guys who were shooting Vicki's pretty titties and stupid onion.

About ten women had realistic chances of winning the Reboul Classic, and of them, only Vicki failed to make par on the first two holes. She barely missed putts from twenty and twelve feet, then turned in our general direction and mouthed profanities I didn't think she even knew.

"Her bogey puts her behind Angela Stanford, Michelle Wie, Kit Manley and Nikki Garrett." Helene shook her head. "I can't believe she missed those two easy putts. Unreal. Outrageous."

I said, "Remember: 'It ain't over till it's over.'"

She rolled her eyes. "Thank you, Yogi Berra."

41

The nonmales kept on cheering for Kit Manley, and at times they sounded like a gang of hardhats making zoo noises at some office cutie walking past a construction zone: "Hubba hubba, baby!" and "Get it in there for Momma!"

"Not exactly the kind of cheerleading I remember from Oliver Johnson Secondary School back in Bayporte," I told Helene.

"I'm sure Vicki and Kit are finding it very embarrassing," she replied. "Kit doesn't know those women and I'm sure she'd love it if they picked on someone else. I'd love it, too. I'm about ready to strangle those bitches. Right now, I could use a Buspar."

But just then Vicki sank a putt for a birdie on the seventh hole. It put her ahead of Kit Manley and a stroke behind Angela Stanford and Michelle Wie. Nikki Garrett had bogeyed a couple of times and fallen out of contention.

"Vicki," Helene said, "is going to win this tournament. I don't know how, but she will do it. There's just something in the way she's playing that says, 'Mum, I'm going to win this thing.'"

"Should I put that in writing?" I asked.

"Better wait a bit."

In retrospect, I can see that, after nine holes, Vicki was in a four-way tie for the lead. She and Kit Manley managed to get even-par scores after the front nine while Angela Stanford and Michelle Wie each finished one under. I got even more confused because Vicki and Kit played ahead of Angela and Michelle, so I just stood there and watched them play it out.

The tenth hole was a long, narrow piece of real estate lined with palm trees and bunkers surrounding the green.

"I hate this one," Helene muttered. "Vicki's not crazy about it, either. She's whacked it into the rough a few times already, you know."

"I know."

But this time she took care of business with it, just as she'd done her thing with my MacBook Pro in New Mexico.

She put her ball on the tee and hit a moon shot of nearly 300 meters, then used an iron and hit her ball so perfectly that it struck the flag and bounced away before stopping twenty feet from the cup. She insisted on playing through and made the twenty-foot putt as if it were a twenty-incher.

The crowd made plenty of noise over Vicki's golf prowess, and Helene giggled almost as much as she did when watching Inderjit Dhaliwal chop away at a stubborn ball.

But we stopped cheering a few moments later, when Vicki hit her next tee shot well past the flag.

"Now she's showing off," said Helene. "That's her biggest flaw as a golfer. Maybe her only flaw."

Vicki, perhaps pumped so full of adrenalin that she could not help herself, signaled for her putter from Huey, who after a few moments of shaking his head, shrugged and handed it over.

Vicki hit the ball, again too hard, and it went at least twenty feet past the cup.

Helene glared at me, as if I'd put a hex on her kid.

If I appeared unperturbed by what I had just seen, if I even seemed a bit smug, I had a good reason for feeling complacent. As hard as I'd cheered for the kid, I'd cheered even harder for my story, and Vicki had given me all the material I needed.

She had battled her way back into the Reboul Classic, and I felt sure she had become a cinch for the *CS* cover. I thought, *It'll be terrific if she wins, but it will be OK if she loses, too. Nothing to be ashamed of, an eighteen-year-old golfer losing the tournament towards the end—indeed, in the final minutes—to a player like Angela Stanford or Kit Manley.*

Helene turned to me and said, "OK, Clancy, here's the deal. You're a big-shot sportswriter, so you know about these things. Here's my question: How in hell can someone like Vicki, with her skill and talent, have such an easy time on the hard holes and a hard time on the easy ones?"

"That's easy," I told her. "It's called 'golf.'"

42

As Kit Manley, with much cursing and frustration, struggled to make a bogey on the seventeenth hole—four hundred yards, a par four—Vicki teed up and hit her ball so well that it ended up on the green, maybe two dozen feet from the stick. From there, she finessed it into the cup. The crowd gasped.

"Do you know why she did that?" Helene asked me, grabbing my arm. "Do you?"

"Tell me."

"Because she can."

"I see."

"And do you know what she's going to do after she wins this thing?"

I shrugged. "Go to Disneyland?"

"No, she's going to buy a black BMW."

"Nice for her."

Ronny Cyrus, my writer pal, had joined us. He said, "Clancy, you could make that your lead:

'Canadian chick wants a black Beemer.'"

"Actually, here's my lead: 'I have seen the future of women's golf, and its name is Vicki Vachon.'"

Ronny rolled his eyes and said, "Thank you, Jon Landau." Then, "You should get her into *Playboy*. I'm sure they would love to do a pictorial of her, with that rack…"

"Watch it, fella." Helene sneered at him. "That's my daughter you're talking about. Nice girls don't do things like that."

"Nice girls do that all the time," Ronny said, cackling. "That's why *Playboy* is so popular: Nice girls posing with wide-open beavers."

"Well," Helene retorted, "*my* nice girl is keeping *her* privates closed and covered."

"Maybe we should just watch the rest of this golf match," I said. "She hasn't actually won it yet."

"Good idea," said Helene. "No more talking about my daughter's rack and beaver, OK?"

…

Vicki and Kit Manley stood together at the eighteenth

hole, a long expanse with trees to the left and an out-of-bounds area to the right. Kit's lips seemed to move constantly and Vicki nodded like a bobblehead.

We walked along the ropes till we reached the green. "Vicki should play it safe here," I said. "Aim for a bogey-five. Remember, she has a two-shot lead."

Helene shook her head. "But what if Kit birdies? That would force a playoff. No, Vicki isn't about playing it safe. She wants to say to this golf course, 'You are my bitch. You will do as I say.'"

"More power to her," I said.

Then we fell silent as Vicki hit her ball over a hundred yards, straight down the middle of the fairway, to the edge of the green.

"Nice," I said. "Very nice indeed."

"More than nice," Helene said. "Wonderful. Magnificent."

"I stand corrected. I don't think there's anything she can do now to botch it up."

"She won't botch it up," said Helene. "Not Vicki Vachon."

The mum had it right. Vicki took out her putter and hit it hard, but away from the cup. The crowd groaned at what seemed to be a very poor putt, then oohed and aahed as the ball, as if by magic, began rolling towards the cup. It kept going, and going, and finally settled a foot from the cup. Kit Manley, who was also on the green, came over and gave Vicki a hug and a pat on the back, then pointed at her and applauded. The crowd, understanding Kit's cue, joined in.

"Isn't she unreal?" Helene exclaimed, throwing her arms around me. "Isn't she awesome?"

She didn't give me a chance to answer. She sealed my lips with the best kiss I'd had since our last makeout session.

Vicki hurried over to her ball, tapped it into the cup and pumped her fist into the air a couple of times before jumping into the arms of her caddy. Other girl golfers rushed to her side with open bottles of discount-store champagne. One girl, because of Vicki's height, jumped onto another's shoulders to pour bubbly over the champ's head. A couple of girls, laughing hard, poured champagne down the front of Vicki's shirt, as if for a wet T-shirt contest.

I pulled up a section of the rope a bit, to make it

easier for Helene to get under it. Ronny Cyrus, Helene and I walked over to Vicki and the others, the three of us pointing at our press credentials to prevent the security people running towards us.

Vicki, spotting Helene, dashed over and threw herself into her mum's arms. The two women said nothing for the longest time; they just held each other tight as the tears stream down their faces.

"This," Helene said finally, "has been about the most exciting week *I've* ever had."

"Come here, Clancy," Vicki said, pulling me into their embrace. To her mother, she said, "Mum, let's go looking at cars next week. I think I want a Beemer, fully loaded, GPS, everything."

"OK, sweetie. Whatever you say."

Then Vicki left us and jogged over to the scorer's tent, accepting high fives from fans along the way.

43

As soon as Vicki went to sign her scorecard and make the Reboul Classic a done deal, three men approached Helene. They all hurried, although they tried to look casual, and they were all sports agents who wanted her to get Vicki to sign with them and make them rich.

"Hi, Helene," said Bert Levenson.

"Congratulations," said Danny Hewitt.

"Long time, no see," said Sneaky Gresham.

Each tried to hand her an envelope, but she refused them all.

"Time for that stuff later," Helene told the men. "Whatever we may have said to each other earlier is no longer valid. Vicki has just won three consecutive majors. Her stock is now significantly higher than it used to be."

"But I have *such* a great deal for you," said Sneaky Gresham. "I can provide you with a tax accountant, traveling companion, investment specialists, caddy—"

"She already has a caddy and I do all those other things for her."

"Good to know." Sneaky Gresham sneered at the contract as he put it into his coat pocket. "I thought it sucked anyway, but my boss insisted on giving it to you."

"I have a better deal for you," said Danny Hewitt. "The girl needs a golf coach, a clothing expert and a spiritual adviser—"

"Oh?" I interjected. "Is Ramtha available?"

"Funny, Clancy," Danny said. "Glad you're here."

"I was being serious," I told him. "She needs a guru of some kind."

"Thanks for your input," Danny said. He looked at Sneaky. "Oh, the other golf rags are here now. We'll get more coverage."

Helene turned to Bert Levenson. "Your silence makes me uncomfortable, Bert."

"Sorry."

"Well, since you're saying very little right now, I'll say a few things. Vicki and I are going away for a couple of weeks to unwind. You have my iPhone number and email address. Give us a week and then contact me and I'll start talking business with all of you guys."

"What do you mean by 'all of you guys'?"

She shrugged, "Just what I said. I have every agent around wanting to represent Vicki. We need to decide which of you guys will get the privilege of making Vicki and me wonderfully stinking rich."

"I see," said Danny Hewitt.

"Also," Helene continued, "I think you probably remember a few years back, when Shari Vollet turned pro as soon as she was old enough to drive. She signed with Rogers Blumenthal. She hadn't won a damned thing, but she was good-looking and the potential to become a perfectly adequate golfer. That agency promised her close to twenty million dollars in her first year, even if she did nothing special as a golfer."

"Yes," said Ronny. "I remember that story, because I wrote it."

"They were idiots," said Danny Hewitt. "Rogers Blumenthal is a talent agency for actors. They don't know about handling athletes."

"Still," Helene said, "I want you to remember that when we talk again really soon. Until then, I will leave you with my favorite movie line. It's only four words."

"Well...?" the agents asked in unison.

Show me the money! Helene mouthed, doing a funky little dance.

A few minutes later, the agents dispersed, all of them frowning, as if they hadn't expected to hear what Helene told them. She looked up at the leaderboard for the longest time, her eyes wide and bright with maternal pride and satisfaction. Vicki's name stood above everyone else's: Kit Manley, Martha Stanford, Michelle Wie. The Canadian kid had beaten the very best in ladies' golf.

"Nice sight," said Ronny Cyrus.

"Beautiful," replied Helene.

"I'll have my photographer take a picture of it for you."

She smiled. "Thanks."

"I have to go write my story," I told them.

"I'll join you and Vicki," said Helene, "right after they give her the trophy."

"Clancy," Ronny Cyrus said, "I think I have a few good ideas for your lead."

"Gee, Ronny," I retorted, "that's mighty white of you, but I think I can manage on my own."

44

My MacBook Pro lay open, my cup of coffee sat hot and fresh for the moment. The problem was, I couldn't think of one damn decent way of starting my story. My muse had flown by and sat on my shoulder many times over the years while I sat taking a shit. Why had she chosen *now* to be aloof?

The other writers ground out their copies, made calls to clarify this or that, asked each other questions, swore at their laptops and deadlines. In other words, they stayed busy.

I had already written most of my story; I just needed a lead. The entire story would be two thousand words. I had to come up with 600 or so new ones, to go at the top.

Those words had to be mine, not anyone else's. Back east in Toronto, they would be mostly gone for the day. Good for me; I've always wanted to avoid giving my editors at *CS* enough time to goof up my work.

A few times, I've naively submitted my stories to those humorless bastards at *CS*, and when my pieces became available for public consumption, the editors had stripped my work of all its wit, charm and eloquence, and I felt ashamed to have my byline attached to it. If I had been up in Toronto at the time, I would have cracked some skulls.

I slurped my coffee as it cooled off, craved a Player's Light and wondered about the best way to tell the world about Vicki's three consecutive tournament victories—the last of which happened to be a major.

Vicki, the first teenager ever to create such interest in women's golf, had joined an elite group of winners in what I persisted in calling the Diefenbaker Classic. Nancy Lopez, Annika Sorenstam and a handful of others. Not that anyone really gave a shit except folks like me.

I sighed, and, feeling uninspired, kept hitting the keys and soon had a thoroughly unremarkable story about a young woman who deserved a better journalistic treatment than what I had written, which concerned itself much more with how she filled out her bikini and lit up a golf course with her smile than with her golfing prowess.

I hit a couple of keys and sent it off to Toronto.

There. Boom. Done.

Vicki, still in the interview room, sat behind a bunch of microphones and a huge replica check. A trophy, beside the replica, looked like a misshapen golf club, but I couldn't be sure.

I hurried over to hear the remaining few minutes of her Q-and-A session when Helene caught up with me.

"Clancy," she said, "we have something to talk about when you're done writing your story."

"Already done."

"Really?" Her eyes grew wide. "How can you write so fast?"

I shrugged. "It's journalism. The story writes itself, mostly. I just have to organize the facts."

We went to a secluded little area near the pressroom. She lit a cigarette and asked, "Clancy, do you *really* have to live in Bayporte?"

"No. We have correspondents elsewhere. But I've been in Bayporte all my life. Why do you ask?"

She took a deep breath. "How about you move down to Florida?"

"You mean so I would be near you'?"

"Yes. Vicki and me."

"I don't have a green card," I told her. "I couldn't afford it. I can't afford Bayporte anymore, either, but I've been there all my life."

She waved me off. "You would live with us in our house. I have a nice big bed. You could work from there and the airport is close by in case you needed to leave town. We could make it work."

I snapped my fingers. "Just like that, eh?"

"Well, why not? You could travel with us and we would go with you. We would be a family."

"Vicki likes the idea?" I asked her.

Helene nodded. "She said, 'Don't let that bugger get away, Mum.'"

"Oh, well, I guess that settles it." I put my arms around her and we kissed for the longest time, forgetting about the rest of the world and all its troubles.